WOLF DEVOTED

ENSNARED BY THE PACK: BOOK 6

TESSA COLE

Gryphon's Gate Publishing

Wolf Devoted
by Tessa Cole

AUDREY

"IF YOU'RE NOT FIGHTING, FOLLOW LUCIUS AND AUDREY," Cyrus yelled as he yanked off his shirt, revealing his broad, muscular chest and powerful arms.

And at any other time, I'd have appreciated his physique — despite him not being romantically interested in me — but with the panicked people rushing closer and the deadly grimalkins right behind them, all I could think about was saving as many lives as I could.

Except that only added frustration to my fear. I couldn't fight the grimalkins, not without a wolf form. Sure, I'd fought them twice before, but only because I'd had no other choice, and I knew just how lucky I'd been to make it out alive.

Which meant the best I could do was help ensure the Mountain and Sea Alliance delegates and their aides were safe. The last thing this horrible situation needed was a political incident on top of it.

"Stick with Lucius," Bishop said to me as he, too, pulled off his shirt. "Make sure no one gets separated."

"Cohnal," Representative Folmar said to the gryphon shifter beside me. "Watch their backs."

Then she shifted into her gryphon form, not caring that she destroyed her clothes in the process.

For a second, no longer than two quick pounds of my heart, I stared at her. In my realm, everyone thought gryphon shifters were extinct or had never existed, but about a dozen feet away stood a majestic creature with the body of a lion and the wings and head of an eagle.

With a piercing cry, she spread her massive wings and leaped into the air, skimming over the heads of the fleeing people and landing on one of the grimalkins.

Cyrus extended his claws from his fingertips and howled, calling his warriors — the sound strange coming from his human throat — then he plunged into the fray. Without hesitation, Bishop followed him, and I could feel his ferocious determination to protect me and his pack racing through our mating bond.

"This way," Lucius called out as he waved toward an alley beside him that sat between some of the semi-permanent market stalls.

He was an older man, his hair gray and deep laugh lines around his eyes and mouth, but I didn't doubt he was still the warrior he'd been when he retired as hunt-master to become the pack's top advisor and diplomat.

A third of the Alliance delegates rushed to follow him, while the others drew their swords or extended their claws, or — in the case of the Dedearc who were covered in scales, already had claws, and were all bigger than Cyrus — just rushed to stop the grimalkins.

But even as everyone ran forward, more grimalkins appeared.

The wave of terrified people surged around the warriors who twisted and turned, trying to move against the flow, and a second later, the wall of people was headed toward me.

Audrey, Lucius said in my head, jerking my attention back to the delegates and reminding me of my duty.

All of them were in the alley, and while I could hesitate for another few moments and let some of the men, women, and children fleeing the grimalkins go ahead of me, that would separate me from the delegates, and my alpha had given me an order.

I scrambled after the group and Cohnal hurried after me.

The alley wasn't long, only six stalls deep before we raced onto a slightly wider road. But that only meant everyone who'd run through the various alleys between the stalls converged on the street, turning into one big horde.

Children screamed and cried, some half shifted unable to control their form while afraid. Men and women who weren't taking care of terrified children or teens, ran with their claws extended, watching for danger to protect those who couldn't protect themselves.

Still, even with an eighth of the horde calm and on

guard, it was chaos. A literal human stampede. One wrong move, one trip, and someone would be crushed to death before anyone could stop it. And while the road was relatively smooth, Stonehaven was built on the rocky slopes at the bottom of a mountain. There were ramps and steps everywhere.

Beside me, a lanky teen boy, probably around fourteen or fifteen, who was desperately trying to carry a much younger child whose form kept shifting between toddler and wolf, tripped.

Cohnal grabbed the back of his collar and yanked him up before he could be knocked completely to the ground by someone else. Except the child shifted into her wolf at the last minute and tumbled from the teen's arms just as he righted himself.

"Jolie!" the teen screamed.

I lunged for the child who tried to jerk out of the way of someone else's feet and ended up getting kicked deeper into the mob.

The child yelped, tiny, heartbreaking noises that I could somehow hear over the pounding feet, screaming, and crying. My pulse lurched as she tried to avoid getting trampled and I heaved against the flow.

Someone slammed into my side, twisting me around and bumping me into someone else. I jerked out of the way before crashing into another person, but everyone was too close together. Heavy feet smashed my toes, while more bodies bumped into me, ricocheting me like a pinball.

Somehow, I cut sideways and reached the child, who'd curled into a tight ball in a desperate attempt to protect herself. Fury and fear churned in a nauseating mix in my stomach as I scrambled to pick her up.

Someone ahead of me screamed and a large man slammed into me. He fell, creating some space in the horde, and I grabbed a handful of fur and yanked the child into my arms.

"You—" he snarled at me as he leaped to his feet. Then he saw the wolf pup in my arms and he gave me a tight nod.

He moved to step closer, possibly to protect us, but the crowd surged, suddenly changing direction, and forced us apart. More screams sounded, desperate and afraid, and a massive gryphon leaped into the air.

Shit. Everyone was running in every direction, slamming into each other, desperate to get away from the grimalkin that I couldn't see but knew was about to have a gryphon attacking it.

I jerked my attention around, trying to find the delegates, but I wasn't tall, a little shorter than average in height, and couldn't see anyone.

Shit shit shit.

The pup in my arms, still curled in a tight ball, whimpered. My first priority was the child's safety. I needed to find the fastest way out of the crowd, and it didn't matter if that brought me closer to or took me farther from the delegation.

A woman carrying two wailing babies slammed into

me, heading the way we'd come, and I curled protectively around the pup as I stumbled after her. But someone else hit me from behind, shoving me hard. I lost my balance and the crowd surged around me.

Someone tried to help me stand but was bumped away by others. Another person tripped over me but managed to keep her balance before righting herself. She didn't even turn to look at who she'd tripped over. She just kept running.

The wind suddenly shifted, and the heavy, foul stench of a grimalkin washed over me, along with the cloying reek of blood. The beast was close. I had to move. Now.

I elbowed a man about to crash into me, earning an angry glare, and heaved to my feet.

The grimalkin roared, the sound so close I was afraid to look behind me. Then two more answered, just as close.

Cohnal screeched and one of the roars turned desperate, but I didn't know how powerful a gryphon was. I'd seen firsthand that one grimalkin was challenging for a couple of shifters unless they were powerful alphas. The black dog-like creatures moved like tigers and had feline-sharp claws. Cohnal might be able to take down one, since his alpha power was strong, but I wasn't going to bet that he could take down three by himself.

I heaved to the edge of the crowd and slipped into one of the extremely narrow passages between some of the wooden market stalls, praying that this time a grimalkin wouldn't be hot on my heels. The space was so tight I had to turn sideways and hold the pup above my head to squeeze through, and there was no way I was going to be able to turn my head to see if one of the monsters was behind me.

My pulse pounding, my breath short sharp gasps, I hurried to the thin rectangle of light ahead of me, careened out the other side, and almost crashed into the rear end of a grimalkin.

AUDREY

I SKIDDED TO A STOP AT THE LAST MINUTE BEFORE I HIT THE grimalkin, the pup in my arms whimpering, just as a large gray wolf as big as Knox lunged at it.

"Audrey!" a feminine voice screamed.

I scrambled away from the fight and scanned the area. I stood at the edge of a small courtyard similar to the one where I'd found a grimalkin toying with those kids in my first grimalkin encounter.

But unlike that one where there were two ways in and out, this courtyard only had one — since squeezing between market stalls didn't count. However, this one had buildings that faced the courtyard, offering not just a place to hide but a possible back door leading to a different, safer street.

Quinn stood at the open door of a squat, one-story building with an older man ushering a group of children inside.

The wolf fighting the grimalkin dug his teeth into the beast's throat, making it howl and rake its claws through the wolf's stomach. But the wolf—

No, Zavier. Somehow, I could tell by the feel of his stuttering, straining alpha power that Zavier was the wolf.

Zavier held on despite the blood rushing from his stomach and spilling onto the stone ground. He viciously wrenched his head to the side and tore his teeth through the grimalkin's throat.

The beast collapsed, but so, too, did Zavier.

Quinn screamed and raced toward him, and so did I.

"Get them inside," she yelled over her shoulder at the older man as she dropped to her knees beside Zavier. "Don't shift. It's too serious."

I knelt at her side. "We have to get him inside, too."

I didn't know if grimalkins were attracted to the scent of blood or not, but I wasn't going to risk it.

"I have an elixir," the man called out.

Tears streamed down Quinn's cheeks and her breathing had turned short and sharp. She scrambled to put pressure on Zavier's wounds, but they were too big for her small hands — hands that were even smaller than mine.

"Quinn!" I barked, my pulse *thu-thudding* softly. "I can't move him by myself."

Her gaze jerked up to mine, her bright blue eyes watery and filled with fear.

"We just need to keep him alive long enough for help

to get to us," I said, and I put down the pup and turned my attention to the quivering child. "Get into the house with the others. I'm right behind you."

The pup darted across the courtyard and I dug my fingers into Zavier's thick fur, grabbing one of his front legs as close to his torso as I could. I didn't want to hurt him any more than he already was, but he was as big as Bishop and Knox in their wolf form and probably just as heavy.

"Sorry," I murmured to him as I braced my legs to start dragging him.

Tell Quinn... he gasped in my mind. *Tell her...*

"Tell her yourself," I hissed. "No one is dying today."

"Right!" Quinn replied, sudden determination hardening her expression, and she grabbed Zavier's other front leg.

Together, we hauled him across the courtyard, leaving a sickeningly large blood smear on the ground, pointing directly to our hiding spot.

Once inside, the older man shut the door and locked it then hurried to a tall metal cabinet and pulled out an elixir.

Quinn and I dragged Zavier to a corner in the back of the room underneath a large metal worktable and fed him the elixir. It wouldn't work quickly, but hopefully, it would be enough to help his shifter-enhanced healing stabilize him long enough for him to get medical attention.

"I don't have a lot of clean towels here," the man said,

taking a small stack from a nearby shelf and handing them to Quinn.

"It's all right," Quinn replied, placing them over Zavier's wounds. "Thanks, Jaxon."

"Anything for you, sweetheart," he replied.

She applied pressure, making Zavier huff in pain, and, much to my surprise, a few of the braver children added their tiny hands, helping her to put pressure on most of his injuries.

With Zavier taken care of as best as possible, given the situation, I straightened and took stock of what was around, not wanting to bet we were safe with only a wooden door and the glass in the windows keeping the grimalkins out.

The building was a single-room smithy without a back door. A blazing-hot fire in a blacksmith's forge burned on the opposite wall from us and close to it were two large anvils and three sturdy worktables. The rest of the space was filled with raw ore, and metal everything: cabinets, stools, a handful of knives and daggers, hoes, rakes, shovels, pots, pans, a plethora of tools, and two dozen wrought-iron fence posts. All of the fence posts were an inch round and half of them had points attached to one end.

It looked like I'd found another makeshift spear, and if the soldering or whatever Jaxon the blacksmith had done to secure the tips held, the fence posts would make better spears than my stick with a point.

I grabbed a post from the rack at the back of the room

then pressed myself against the cool stone wall beside one of the front windows so I could peek out and watch for danger.

"You're definitely living up to the rumors, alpha," Jaxon said as he took a similar position at the other window.

His voice was firm, and his medium-level alpha power rolled off him in small, stuttering waves, revealing his heightened emotions, but I didn't get the impression he disliked me. In fact, for a second, I thought I saw respect in his eyes before he turned his attention out the window.

I wasn't sure if he'd always felt that way, or if seeing me, a shifter who couldn't shift, grab a weapon and stand ready to fight to protect Quinn, Zavier, and fifteen kids under the age of ten had changed his opinion of me... and I wasn't going to ask him about the rumors. Even if there were a few good ones, I was sure most were bad.

"Just trying to do the right thing," I replied, scanning the courtyard.

It was empty, but somewhere out of sight, people screamed and yelled, and it felt more like the calm before the storm.

My pulse pounded, and waves of determination, anger, and fear roared through my mating bonds, making me pray that my guys were safe. I tried to keep my bonds locked tight, not wanting my own fear to distract them. In a fight like this, just a flicker of a distraction could be deadly.

Then the sides of the two wooden stalls I'd squeezed

through to get to the courtyard shook and a small, terrified wolf bolted out from between them. My muscles tensed, my body about to jump to the door to let the wolf in.

But before I could move, the stalls burst apart. Wood pieces, bright material, and books flew everywhere and two grimalkins pounced on the wolf.

The first sank its teeth into the wolf's back, drawing a desperate, terrified howl, while the other dug its claws into the wolf's side, trying to wrench it away from the first one. They snarled and roared at each other, their fight tearing the wolf in half before I could even think to scream.

I clamped a hand over my mouth, afraid to make any noise that might attract the monsters. Bile burned the back of my throat and tears stung my eyes. It had happened so fast. Logically I knew I wouldn't have had time to save whoever it was, but my soul screamed with fury that I'd been useless.

That had been a member of my pack — *mine!* — and the wildness deep inside me howled that I needed to protect what was mine.

One of the children started crying. She might not have been able to see what had happened — thank goodness — but she'd heard that wolf's death cry and the grimalkins' growls.

"Shh shh shh," Quinn hissed, her gaze darting to mine, her eyes wide with fear, before she turned to the child and tucked her against her side. "We have to stay quiet."

All the children nodded, tears rolling down their cheeks, their bodies quivering, and half of them clamped their hands over their mouths, trying to stifle their sobs.

I jerked my attention to the horror in the courtyard as the beasts fought over the wolf's corpse. They snarled and swatted at each other, then the larger one batted the slightly smaller one hard, sending it skidding across the courtyard toward the smithy.

I sucked in a sharp breath and held it, my rushing pulse filling my ears.

Don't look our way.

Don't notice us.

Don't notice the blood leading straight to our door.

Please.

The smaller grimalkin leaped to his feet, shaking off the blow, and turned away from the smithy.

Yes. That's it.

Both of you leave and run into a pack of hunters.

The large grimalkin snarled at the smaller one and a heavy, skin-crawling wave of power — far too similar to the ominous power I'd felt in Anakar — slammed into me as the smaller grimalkin shrank back.

My pulse stuttered with realization.

Holy shit!

The grimalkins had alpha power... and somehow, I could sense it?

One of the kids whimpered, making me wonder if

she, too, could feel the strange power, and the smaller grimalkin's head, which had dipped in submission to the bigger one, snapped around. Its gaze locked on the blood trail and its ears tipped forward. That drew the larger one's attention and in unison, they both zeroed in on the door.

Oh shit.

AUDREY

With a roar, the large one charged past the smaller one and slammed itself against the door, the wood cracking with the impact. Desperate, I shot my gaze around, looking for something to block the entrance.

Another crash and wood flew everywhere. I jerked away to protect my face from the shrapnel, right in the direction of the shattering window.

Flicks of pain burst across my face, neck, and arms, and my pulse lurched. I wrenched my spear up before I'd fully opened my eyes, the tip skimming across the smaller grimalkin's rough hide, not even drawing a scratch.

The beast roared, its foul scent flooding my nostrils, and bounded toward Quinn, Zavier, and the children.

"No," I yelled, my pulse *thu-thudding*, my wildness roaring to the surface.

The children screamed, the group shrinking and

pressing closer to the wall as if that would protect them, and Quinn leaped to her feet, her fingers extended into claws.

I didn't know how much fighting experience she had, but I doubted it was a lot. She was a schoolteacher and was going to get torn apart like the dead wolf in the courtyard.

I rammed my spear into the grimalkin's side, breaking flesh and drawing blood. With a howl that sounded more angry than hurt, the beast turned to me, wrenching itself free from my spear.

Fuck me.

Fear tore through me but so did my wildness. I'd killed one of these monsters before and I could do it again. I had to. Quinn and those children were counting on me.

More heavy skin-crawling power crashed over me as the grimalkin leaped at me, but my own power surged, batting it away as if it were nothing, and I aimed my spear right for the monster's mouth. It had worked the last time with just a broken stick and it was going to work now.

But the beast wrenched his head to the side at the last minute, and my spear skidded uselessly across its hide — because, of course, the damn tip was only more or less sharp at the point since it was a fence post and not an actual weapon.

Its head slammed into my chest and sent me tumbling across the room, right into the fight between the larger grimalkin and Jaxon, who'd shifted into his wolf form.

The large beast swiped at me, and I rolled out of the way, slamming into a table leg and sending a box of thick nails crashing to the floor.

Jaxon charged at the beast, trying to bite its throat, but the grimalkin swatted at him, forcing him to twist mid-air to avoid its claws. Except he wasn't fast enough and the beast slashed Jaxon's side.

Too-bright blood stained his pale gray coat and he howled as the grimalkin attacked.

My heart pounded hard, fear and ferocity surging through my veins. Screaming, I grabbed my make-shift spear — which had tumbled from my grip when I'd landed in the middle of Jaxon's fight.

The grimalkin swung its large blocky head toward me, its foul breath filling the space between us as it surged toward me. I wrapped my fingers around the fence post, wrenched the weighty piece of metal around toward the beast, and shoved the pointed tip inside the monster's mouth.

Just like the last time, the spear hit something then *popped* through. Blood gushed from the grimalkin's mouth, its eyes glazed over, and it crashed on top of me.

Hell, yes!

One down. One more to go.

I half shoved half squirmed out from under the grimalkin that was larger than Cyrus in his wolf form and wrenched on my spear.

Stuck.

I couldn't even get it to budge.

Something crashed on the other side of the room, and I yanked my attention to Quinn and the kids. With her enhanced shifter strength, she'd pushed over the heavy metal table the children and Zavier had been hiding under, creating a short wall, and now stood in front of it, blocking the smaller grimalkin's way.

Except even with her claws and canines extended, it was ridiculous to think she could stand her ground against the monster. She wasn't even five feet tall and probably didn't weigh a hundred pounds.

The beast lunged at her, and Jaxon flew past me, ramming his body against the grimalkin and knocking it off balance.

I scrambled to my feet, raced to the rack at the back of the room, and grabbed another fence post.

With a roar, the grimalkin swatted at Jaxon and he stumbled to the side, more bright splashes of blood staining his fur, making my pulse stutter.

Quinn leaped forward and slashed her claws across the grimalkin's snout, drawing its attention back to her. Its heavy skin-crawling power rolled over me, making my stomach churn, and the muscles in its back legs bunched, preparing to attack.

I wasn't going to get to it in time to distract it from attacking Quinn... Except that was all I needed to do. Distract it. I only needed a second, long enough to join the fight and help them.

I threw my fence post. It hit the stone floor with a clatter a good three feet before it reached the grimalkin and skidded forward, stopping between its feet.

Swell.

But at least the beast wrenched its head toward me instead of attacking Quinn. I grabbed another spear and barreled toward it. Except before I reached it, another grimalkin and a large gray wolf flew through the already shattered window, knocking more shards from the frame and sending them flying in all directions.

The two of them rolled midair — the wolf with its teeth in the grimalkin's throat and the grimalkin trying to get its claws in the wolf's belly.

With a *thud,* they skidded across the floor, the grimalkin on top using its weight to bear down on the wolf and drive the wolf headfirst into an anvil.

Stunned, the wolf's grip on the grimalkin's throat released and the grimalkin rose to tear into the wolf with its claws.

The wildness inside me roared to the surface. I howled a war cry and charged at it. The beast jerked its head up and I rammed my spear into its eye.

Roaring, the grimalkin leaped away from the wolf— No, Finn. The dazed, bleeding wolf on the floor was Finn, Stonehaven's Watch Commander.

I scrambled out of the way of the beast's claws and slammed into the side of the other grimalkin.

Thankfully, Jaxon snapped at the smaller one's throat,

making it swipe at him. He barely managed to get out of the way, but without a doubt he'd saved my life.

The new grimalkin lunged for me, and I heaved to the side, desperate to avoid getting pinned between the two monsters. But the grimalkin kept pressing its attack, forcing me to scramble out of the way, knocking over stands and buckets, scattering tools and metal things, and not giving me a chance to fight back.

That made the wildness inside me furious. My pulse roared and my heart pounded violent thuds that reverberated through me.

Finn groaned and the eyelid of his one visible eye fluttered. Blood trickled onto the floor by his stomach, but it wasn't gushing. Which meant he wasn't about to die, and if Jaxon could fight with worse injuries, so could Finn... because there was no way I was going to get lucky two more times and kill both of the grimalkins myself.

"Finn!" I barked, my wildness crashing through me.

I rolled over a worktable, the grimalkin's claws tearing the bottom half of my dress to shreds.

Fuck fuck fuck.

"Finn!" I barked again as the beast leaped over the table, forcing me to scramble out of reach.

My back hit the wall beside the forge, the stone searingly hot against my bare skin, and I jerked away, knocking over a bucket of ash. My thigh bumped a metal poker, its tip in the fire, and I grabbed it. I smashed the poker against the grimalkin's nose and raced back around the table.

The beast roared with pain and its horrible stomach-churning skin-crawling power slammed into me.

This grimalkin was a lot more powerful than the one I'd killed, and my knees started to buckle in submission.

But my wildness surged out of me in response, over-whelming the grimalkin's power. The beast shrank back with its teeth bared, red light flashing in its eyes, and fury pouring from it as its alpha power battled mine.

My stomach roiled and bile burned the back of my throat. Behind me, a wolf howled in agony and Quinn screamed.

"Get. The. Fuck. Up. Finn!" I roared and he lurched to his feet, his eyes wide, the expression almost cartoonish on a wolf. "Help me."

Without hesitation, almost as if he were being controlled, he threw himself at the grimalkin attacking me, giving me a chance to hurry around to the monster's side for my own attack.

But as I got into position, movement in the courtyard caught my attention. Two more grimalkins were barreling toward us.

"You've got to be kidding me," I hissed as my wildness tore through me, bringing with it a ferocious anger.

Mine. This pack was mine and everyone in this smithy was getting out alive.

The grimalkins needed to leave now or die. I didn't know how I'd kill them, but my wildness didn't care about the details. It would tear them to shreds and bathe in their blood.

Furious, I threw the spear at the smaller grimalkin that was about to tear into Jaxon. The weapon miraculously slammed into the beast's eye, tore through its head, and embedded itself in the stone wall behind it.

Power rolled off me in violent ferocious waves and my stomach heaved with something darker... something angrier.

Finn clamped his teeth around the other grimalkin's throat and tore it out with a rush of foul-smelling blood, and I turned my attention to the two grimalkins outside.

They were almost at the smithy. A few more steps and I'd be forced to fight them. Instead, that dark power surged. My stomach cramped with sudden, painful nausea, and the biting acid burn of bile rose up my throat.

The grimalkins' gaze leaped to mine, and I squared my shoulders despite my body's desperate plea to curl inward and protect the agony churning in my stomach.

"Come on, assholes," I snarled under my breath, sending the burn racing over my tongue and out of my mouth in a whisp of black smoke — that could only be from my imagination because of how angry I was.

And right now. I didn't care if I was hallucinating. Whatever kept me strong and ended the threat to the people who were mine.

"I will fucking kill every last one of you." Another whisp of black smoke curled out of my mouth and my stomach cramped, forcing me to suck in rapid breaths before I puked on my feet.

The grimalkins jerked to a stop. Skin-crawling power slammed into me, and I surged my wildness in return, matching their wave with my tsunami. I would crush them, rip them to shreds, and dance on their corpses. Vengeance would be mine, and I'd feast on their flesh and bathe in their blood.

I. Was. Done.

I was done with these monsters terrorizing this pack, hurting the people I'd grown to love, and terrifying children. And I was done with being weak and pathetic. I'd already killed two of these fuckers today. Two more was easy.

I blindly reached behind me, grabbed a fence post, and stormed out the front door to face them.

The grimalkins hunched almost as if they were going to pounce, but then the smaller one shifted back a step.

That's right. Fear me! the something dark and powerful screamed within me. *Die!*

With a roar, I rushed forward, my wildness— No, my *alpha* power pouring off me in giant waves, my stomach cramping, and wisps of black smoke rushing from my mouth.

The bigger grimalkin also hunched, its back legs bunching as if to attack. But that only made me grin... because somehow, I'd lost my mind. Somehow, I was furious enough to believe I could take on two more grimalkins by myself.

"Run or die," the darkness inside me hissed, and, as if

I'd actually commanded them, the two beasts bolted away. "That's right, fuckers!"

Oh, my God!

I'd scared off two grimalkins!

My stomach cramped, wrenching me to my hands and knees, and I threw up a burning mix of bile and black smoke.

KNOX

AUDREY COLLAPSED ONTO HER HANDS AND KNEES AND threw up. Her green dress and pale skin were soaked with blood as if someone had thrown a bucket of it on her, making it hard to tell at a distance how badly she was hurt.

Surely not all of it was hers! But the beautiful gift Bishop had given her to wear when she met the delegates and aides from the alliance was ripped to shreds, so she couldn't have gotten through the fight unscathed.

I'd found her just in time to watch her brandish a fence post, scream, and rush toward two grimalkins like a wild woman. Her alpha power had poured off her in great, destructive waves, nearly flattening me in my wolf form into submission, and I could feel her determination and rage pounding through our mating bond. But I knew none of it would affect the grimalkins. They weren't wolf shifters and our power only affected those of our kind.

My heart had clenched with fear, and my wolf seized control of our body, shoving me so far back into our consciousness it felt like I was looking at the horrific scene in front of me from the end of a long tunnel.

With a ferocious wildness that verged on going feral, my wolf raced toward them even while knowing he wasn't going be fast enough to save her. Except instead of attacking, the grimalkins turned tail, their eyes wide with fear, and bolted toward me. I tensed, but they didn't even look at me. They kept running down the street as if their life depended on it.

My wolf rushed us to Audrey's side, shifted into our human form, and curled protectively around her, clutching her to our chest as she heaved again and spat bile and breakfast onto the ground.

Her pounding power and burning rage shattered into body-shaking horror as her adrenaline vanished and her breath turned into short, sharp gasps, making my wolf growl with rage. Our mate was sick and trembling and those grimalkins were still alive. He needed to tear them apart to ensure her safety... but he also couldn't let her go.

Mine, he snarled over and over again.

Mine and I'd failed her. I hadn't been here to protect her. She'd had to face those two grimalkins—

No, three. A dead grimalkin lay on the other side of the courtyard near the torn-up corpse of one of our packmates. She'd had to deal with three grimalkins and watch that massacre.

And while both my wolf and I recognized that our

mate was powerful, she was still soft and sensitive. She shouldn't have had to face those monsters. I should have been by her side the whole time, not slinking through the shadows, unable to keep her in sight all the time because of the crowded market.

"Audrey," a female called from behind me.

My wolf jerked us around, snarling and baring our human teeth at Quinn as she rushed out of Jaxon's smithy — and my wolf didn't stop snarling when we recognized the woman.

I heaved against my wolf's control, terrified the need to protect our mate would consume both of us and send us into feralness. With the stress of almost losing Bishop so strong in my wolf's memory, it was impossible to keep hold of our base instincts.

Mine.

Mine mine mine.

"Knox, it's okay," Audrey gasped, her small body still trembling in my arms.

"It's not okay," my wolf growled between clenched teeth.

Must protect. Mine.

More footsteps pounded on the ground behind me. More people. More danger.

And while my wolf recognized that the mix of human and wolf steps meant pack and not more grimalkins, it didn't calm him. He raged within my human skin, desperate to shift and take his proper form but also desperate to keep holding her, something we could only do with human arms.

Must protect. Always.

"Knox," she murmured, her voice weak and shaky, making my feralness surge.

She wasn't well. She needed protection. She'd thrown up and that meant something was wrong. Even her emotions were hard to feel, and it wasn't because my wolf was a primal beast walking the edge of becoming a mindless animal and only understood basic emotions. No, she was blocking us out.

The realization squeezed around my heart.

She was blocking *us* out.

Which meant she was hiding something, and with everything I knew about her, it was some kind of injury or weakness.

My wolf wrenched our attention to the road as Nova, two medics, and three hunters in their wolf form raced toward us.

My snarl deepened despite knowing Nova would help.

"Is she hurt?" Nova asked while still a good ten feet away.

"Yes," my wolf growled.

"I'm fine," Audrey said even though she was too pale. "Zavier and Jaxon are inside."

"No," my wolf barked, my power snapping and freezing everyone in place.

A mix of hot emotions flashed through our mating

bond too fast for me to recognize any of them, and Audrey shook her head.

"Zavier and Jaxon first," she insisted.

But my wolf wouldn't release them from our power. He needed them to ensure Audrey's safety... but he also didn't want any of them closer.

The dueling emotions roared within us. Must protect. Must help. Must keep safe. Must care for her.

Fur rippled down my arms and across my cheeks, and my face started to shift, my mouth and nose extending into a snout.

Audrey shook in my arms even while I could sense through our bond that she was trying to get ahold of herself and not set me off.

"Knox," she murmured as she turned into my embrace and pressed her face against my neck. She drew in a deep breath and the comfort she felt from my scent rolled through our mating bond. "You have to let them do their job. Zavier is hurt."

A whisper of fear bled through a crack she'd formed in the block between us, and my chest tightened with both my and my wolf's emotions.

Still ten feet away, Nova and her team trembled in my control.

Safe. I had to keep Audrey safe.

"Please, Knox." A whisper of Audrey's alpha power teased over our skin, not with a demand for my submission but a reassurance that she was strong enough to wait.

My wolf's hold on our body trembled. I surged my consciousness forward, seized control, and released Nova and her team.

"Iris check out Audrey," Nova said, making eye contact with me.

I gave her a tight nod, shoved my nose against the top of Audrey's head, and huffed her scent like an addict in a desperate attempt to stay in control and not rip Iris's throat out.

"Cora with me," Nova finished as she, Cora, and Quinn rushed toward Jaxon's smithy.

"Zavier, Jaxon, and Finn all need medical attention," Audrey said. "I can wait. Iris, go with Nova."

My wolf surged, but Audrey's power grew stronger as well, pushing him back and urging me to calm the fuck down.

"You're hurt." She threw up for fuck's sake. Something was wrong with her.

"Nova, go," Audrey said, her voice stronger. "I've got Knox."

Nova and the medics hurried inside while the three hunters stood guard, watching the narrow road and the destroyed vender stalls. Nova immediately rushed to the back of the building— with Quinn at her side — while Iris and Cora split in opposite directions. Children started to cry and Audrey leaped to her feet.

Blood rolled down her thigh from three deep gashes, and my wolf saw red and surged forward.

"No." He seized her wrist and slammed our power into her, freezing her in place.

"Knox!"

Before she could counter with her own power, he tore the ruined dress from her body and pulled her close to examine her. She had thin cuts on her cheeks and arms, most that had stopped bleeding, a deep slice against her ribs, more on her calf, and half a dozen shallow ones across her back like she'd narrowly escaped the grimalkin's claws.

But before we could drag her to the ground and lick her wounds, Nova yelled to two of the hunters for help. They hurried inside, then the first hunter, Brody, carried out Jaxon, still in his wolf form. He was awake, but his panting was too fast and he'd already bled through the bandages they'd wrapped around him, while Iris, the medic, helped Finn — in his human form — limp into the courtyard. Rough bandages wrapped around my Watch Commander's torso and one thigh, and he too was still bleeding.

A second later, Quinn, her face wet with tears despite her forced calm expression along with fifteen children hurried out followed by Nova and Wade who carried Zavier. He hung limp in Wade's arms, blood dripping from the bandages they'd wrapped around his wolf form, and Audrey's power surged against mine, breaking my hold on her.

"Zavier," she cried out, even as my wolf in our human body pounced on her and pulled her into my arms.

"Stop moving. You're hurt," he snarled.

"I'm fine."

"You're not." I tugged her off her feet and clutched her to my chest.

"If she can stand, she's good enough to get to the hospital," Nova snapped at me. "Come on, we can't waste time."

CYRUS

Folmar pinned another grimalkin, and I sank my teeth in the beast's neck and jerked my head before it could break free. The reek of rotten flesh, mixed with the coppery tang of blood, rushed across my senses, making my stomach heave, but I didn't pause to react, just swung my head to the side, searching for the next grimalkin.

The beasts had been ferocious in their attack, toying and torturing, this pack more aggressive than the pack that had attacked before — not to mention five times the size.

I hadn't seen so many grimalkins in one pack in my life, not even when I'd joined the hunting party to clear out the pack that had threatened Stonehaven five years ago and was responsible for killing my mother and fathers. And these grimalkins smelled and tasted worse than any of the others I'd fought.

The thought tightened my chest for what that meant, for the safety of my pack, and for the safety of one member in particular, and I struggled to stay focused on the job at hand.

But the grimalkins were everywhere. Finn and Deacon were fielding reports from all over the eastern half of the city, and Nova had put out a call for more help, asking anyone with even basic first aid training to go to the hospital so she could pull nurses to her field hospital. We didn't have enough people trained in medicine to deal with this kind of attack. Shifters didn't get sick often, and we healed relatively quickly unless the wounds were too severe or the illness something our natural healing couldn't handle.

And Audrey was in the middle of this disaster.

My wolf threatened to take over and go after her, but I managed to hold him back. She was fine. Lucius wouldn't let anything happen to her.

Except in chaos like this, anything could happen.

Lucius, I mentally called to him, not bothering to be polite and touch his mind first. *Are the delegates safe?*

Was Audrey safe?

We're almost at the hospital, he replied. *Minor scrapes and bruises.*

Good. I clenched my jaw before I could ask about Audrey. She wasn't my mate, not yet, and I had a priority to the pack and our guests.

Audrey got separated from the group, he continued as if

he knew that I desperately needed to know something about her. Except his words sent panic rushing through me. *Cohnal made sure she got away, so I'm sure she's fine.*

But you don't have eyes on her?

Except I already knew he didn't and didn't know of anyone else who did or he would have said so.

Fuck.

My thoughts lurched to mentally connecting with Audrey, but I couldn't. She didn't have telepathy like the rest of my pack. Even if I could speak into her mind, she wouldn't be able to answer me back.

Cyrus, Folmar barked in my head.

I wrenched my attention to her as she tried to leap into the air. But a grimalkin launched itself at her, forcing her to twist out of the way toward another grimalkin.

I tensed, my muscles bunching to rush in and help when one of the merchants shot his lightning weapon.

A blast of terrifying electric power roared from the device, skimming the side of the grimalkin and exploding into a wooden market stall with blankets and towels. Fabric and wood flew everywhere, and small fires littered the area where the stall had been.

The shot at least distracted the grimalkins enough for Folmar to take flight, and I dove for the injured one, snapping my teeth into the softest — but still not that soft — part of the grimalkin's hide, its throat.

The beast roared and dug its claws into my shoulder, but I locked my jaw and hung on, twisting as best I could to avoid its flailing strikes.

I had thirty seconds before the idiot merchant could shoot that nightmare weapon again, and I wanted these two grimalkins dead before he could blow up more of my city.

And fuck me, there were two more of those merchants wreaking havoc out there, fighting alongside the other alliance members.

The grimalkin got a claw into my stomach, raking through my flesh with burning agony, and I wrenched hard with my head. With a pain- and fury-filled roar, the beast shoved me with his shoulder, trying to force me onto my back.

I sank into a low crouch, ignoring the pain screaming through me from the myriad wounds I'd gotten since the fight had begun. I was the alpha.

I. Would. Not. Surrender.

Not even if the monster outweighed me, which this one did.

Folmar screeched, my only warning before she dug her claws into the grimalkin's back, giving me a chance to wrench to the side and kill it.

Folmar, check in with your son, I commanded. *Is he with Audrey?*

Folmar tilted her eagle head to the side, her lion's tail flicking fast and hard against the ground.

I can't reach him.

Bishop. Knox. Where's Audrey? I asked, panic making me pant.

I shouldn't have let her out of my sight. I should

have insisted Bishop stay with her instead of helping the fight. From Finn and Deacon's reports, the grimalkins were all over the east side and she was probably sacrificing herself right now to protect the pack's children.

You can't find her? Bishop asked, his mental voice tight. *She's... It's hard to tell. She's blocking me. All I'm getting are flashes of... fear... and determination.*

Of course, she was determined. That was our mate to a T.

Except she wasn't *our* mate.

Not yet.

Knox, I mentally snapped, desperate to stay focused.

No response.

Knox! I shifted into my human form. I needed to find her. Now! And I couldn't do that as injured as I was.

Exhaustion swept over me, making me stagger because I should have stayed in my wolf form and given my body more time to heal before trying to finish the job with a shift.

Fuck, Knox. Where the hell are you?

He's almost feral, Bishop replied.

Is she alive? Bishop, please. Tell me she's alive. I didn't care if I was showing Bishop how much I needed his mate. To hell with my pride and anything else. She was all that mattered.

Mine, my wolf growled and he surged forward, shoving my consciousness to the back of our body.

Hospital, Knox finally snarled, his mental voice filled

with anger and frustration. *I can't go inside, there are too many people. She says she's fine but—*

A shuddered of alpha power swept over the market.

My wolf jerked me forward, but somehow, I managed to stop us from abandoning our comrades. *Folmar!*

It's clear, she said as if already knowing what I wanted. *Find your mate.*

She's not—

She leveled an unblinking golden eye at me. *I'm old. I'm not dumb.*

With a snarl, my wolf regained control of our body, shifted us into our wolf form, and we bolted down the street. It didn't matter to my wolf that we, the alpha, was racing to the hospital for a woman we hadn't publicly claimed as our mate and wouldn't be able to until we'd squashed the horrible rumors about her.

In that moment, Audrey was all that mattered.

She was mine, the alpha I'd never known I was looking for to help lead our pack. I had to know she was safe.

Sisters! Nova had taken her to the hospital and Knox was all riled up. Audrey was even blocking her emotions from Bishop. That couldn't be good. She had to be hiding something to protect her mates, something she feared would distract them from the fight with the grimalkins.

It didn't matter that I'd done exactly what I suspected she was trying to avoid. I'd abandoned my position, trusting Folmar when she said the area was clear of grimalkins, and was running at full speed.

What the fuck was wrong with me? My mother and fathers had taught me better. Even Audrey knew better. I was the alpha. I had to lead the pack. But my instincts were screaming at me. I had to ensure my mate was safe.

CYRUS

Nova, I mentally called, grateful that I'd spent all that time working to extend how far my telepathy reached.

Busy, she snapped back.

Audrey, I snarled, skidding around a corner and nearly barreling into two of the pack's watchmen.

She's with Molly.

"Not you?" my wolf wanted to roar, but I managed to hold him back, leap over the other wolves, and continue running. If Audrey was in serious condition, Nova would have been with her. Since she wasn't, it meant she felt Audrey's condition was good enough that she could delegate.

Except that thought didn't calm my wolf. Our mate was in the hospital and Knox was freaking out. *Something* had happened to her.

Molly, I said, feeling her mentally jump with surprise. *Audrey.*

I ducked down a side street purposely avoiding Nova's field hospital, my paws pounding on the smoothed-stone road. If Knox said he couldn't go inside that meant Audrey was at the building, not in Sisters Square.

I leaped up five stairs in one bound and rounded another corner, running onto a wider street, the large two-story hospital straight ahead.

Straining my body, I picked up my pace, racing toward the emergency room doors only to find it packed with people.

Fuck.

Alpha, Molly replied. *She said she's a slow healer.*

My heart lurched. Did Molly not believe her? Was necessary medical attention being withheld from my mate.

What haven't you done? I snarled as I reached a side door, shifted, and yanked it open. My alpha power snapped off me, and I knew I'd just hit everyone in the hospital with my lack of control.

Nothing, Molly squeaked. *I mean, everything? I'm treating her like a human. She said it was how I was supposed to.*

Where is she?

In the staff locker room cleaning up so I can finish, Molly replied and I could feel her submitting her will to me even through our telepathic link.

Cleaning up? Did that mean she wasn't hurt that

badly? Or was she being stubborn and Molly didn't want to argue with the mate of two of the pack's alphas?

I hadn't spent a lot of time with Molly, but she'd struck me as a quiet and sensitive nurse. There was no way she'd have stood up against Audrey if my mate had made up her mind about something. Even if Audrey hadn't released her massive alpha power, all she needed was the idea that children were in danger and no one would be able to stop her.

Well, no one except me... maybe.

I raced down the halls toward the locker room, not caring that I was completely naked, and managed to avoid the busier parts of the hospital so I wouldn't be stopped by anyone. The need to get to her and ensure she was okay, that she'd received the right medical care and wasn't going to turn around and do something stupid, overwhelmed all other thoughts.

I barged into the staff locker room, not caring who might be inside. The room, with three rows of lockers and benches, was empty, everyone dealing with the grimalkin emergency. But I could hear a shower running in the shower room and smell Audrey, along with the coppery tang of blood.

Mine, my wolf growled inside me.

He was tired of waiting, tired of having gotten a taste of her twice but denied more. He didn't want to wait until Audrey had shown the rest of the pack what we already knew: that she was our mate and more than strong enough to help lead the pack.

He also didn't think we needed to be careful because someone had tried to kill her and that *someone* could be a member of our pack.

If we claimed her now, it wouldn't draw unwanted attention. It would protect her. Everyone would know not to fuck with what was ours. Claiming her wouldn't paint a bigger target on her back like our human half feared, and so what if someone challenged us to be alpha? We'd force them to submit. We'd force anyone who opposed us because Audrey was mine.

We stormed into the shower room — a single white and blue tiled room with six showerheads — to see our prize partially standing in a stream of water, her eyes shut and her expression tight with worry.

Scratches and bruises covered her perfect body, and two neat rows of stitches curled up her right calf along with another row across her right ribs. Pink water swirled around her feet before running into the drain, and she was going to need to bandage up the wounds that still wept but weren't deemed deep enough for stitches once she'd dried off.

Still, she was the most gorgeous woman I'd ever seen, her features sculpted by a master: delicate cheekbones, small nose, and eyes that could— no *had* captured my soul. Her torso and waist were still too thin from the journey north and her near-deadly heat, but her small breasts and hips were perfect. Hips that would bear me and my brothers the most beautiful babies.

My cock hardened, standing at attention and pointing to my mate.

Mine. Always mine, my soul breathed, and I strode toward her.

"Cyrus," she gasped, curling in on herself, one hand dropping to cover her mound, the other over her pert breasts.

"Don't you dare," my wolf snarled as he seized her wrists, jerked her hands up, and backed her against the tiled wall. "Don't you dare hide from me."

My wolf didn't wait for a response and smashed my lips against hers. She froze, her body tensing as my human half screamed and struggled against my wolf's control. He wanted her submission, wanted to dominate and control her. He wanted to fuck her until she saw stars and screamed with pleasure.

With a growl, he transferred her wrists to one hand, easily holding them, and tugged, stretching her until she was on her toes. Then he grabbed a handful of her wet hair and jerked her head back.

The move drew a throaty gasp and her arousal flooded around me.

So, she liked it a little rough, liked to be dominated. Good.

Of course, that also didn't surprise me. Given how Knox reacted to her, he was probably unhinged when they had sex, and she hadn't run screaming from him yet.

"You like that?" my wolf growled, breaking our kiss and capturing her gaze with mine.

"Cyrus," she gasped again, her pupils fully blown with desire.

My name on her lips, that look in her eyes, and the scent of her arousal threw my wolf into a frenzy.

We smashed our mouth back to hers, yanked her hair, and shoved our tongue into her mouth when she groaned with pleasure. Our other hand raked up and down her body, roughly kneading one breast then the other before pinching and plucking her nipples.

She moaned and panted, kissing me back with a fever that matched my own even while she struggled to break free.

"Cyrus, I want— I want to touch you," she begged.

"No," I snapped and ground my leaking cock against her stomach. "*I'm* in control. Ask again and I'll find a better use for your mouth."

She sucked in a breath. I didn't know if it was to speak or not, but my wolf snapped our power around her and dropped her to her knees.

I slapped my cock against her lips and more arousal thickened the air as her power flickered against mine, teasing and not resisting.

"Open," I commanded.

She obeyed, and I shoved my cock into her, hitting the back of her throat and making her gag. But even then, she didn't fight me, moaning in pleasure instead. She fully submitted, letting me hold her wrists above her in an iron grip and fisting her hair to jerk her head back farther.

My wolf fucked her mouth with hard, fast strokes,

and there wasn't anything I could do to slow him down or soften his thrusts. He needed to brand himself on her body, mind, and soul. He didn't care that she hadn't claimed him with an unprepared mating bond like she had with Knox and Bishop. *He* was going to do the claiming this time because... She. Was. Mine.

Tears rolled down her cheeks and saliva oozed down her chin, but the scent of her arousal kept thickening, turning the mist from the hot shower still running beside us into a heady, enveloping cloud.

She moaned around me, her eyes rolled back in pleasure. I couldn't get enough of her, of her scent, her desire, and I sure as hell couldn't get enough of the feel of her tongue stroking the underside of my cock and the pressure from her swallowing around me while she tried to suck me down.

Hot tingles spread up from the base of my spine and I knew I was on the verge of coming.

With a snarl, I wrenched Audrey up, spun her around, and bent her forward. I seized her hips and plunged my cock into her dripping pussy, the same one she'd flaunted when she'd crawled across the uneven ground beside the healing pool so she could fuck my brother.

She released a throaty moan that went straight to my balls, making them tighten, her breathing ragged pants of need.

Sisters! I'd spent every night since that night in the

pool dreaming of fucking her like this and nothing I imagined came close to how it actually felt.

I pulled her down to her hands and knees, pressed her forehead against the wet tiles, and sat back, savoring my mate in full submission with my cock buried inside her.

Mine. All mine.

Then I jerked my cock out and pounded back into her, drawing another moan of pleasure.

Tremors raced through her body and her walls fluttered around me. She was close. Which was good, because my wolf didn't want to wait for her pleasure. He wanted to pump her full of his seed now now now.

We thrust in and out, again and again, our pace wild and demanding. She gasped and moaned, her trembling growing to the point where she couldn't match my strokes with bucks of her own, but I didn't care. I'd get her there. My wolf might want to breed her and brand our body to hers, but I wanted her soul.

I shifted my angle and hit a spot inside her that made her scream and shake, each stroke taking her higher and higher until every muscle in her body contracted and she wailed her release.

Her cry sent me over the edge and I thrust hard, burying myself as deeply as I could and I erupted inside her. I groaned so loud I was sure anyone in the locker room, hell, probably even the hall beyond would have heard me.

My canines extended and my wolf surged forward,

capturing her small body under us, but panic seized my human half.

We hadn't talked about me claiming her. It wasn't right. No matter how much my wolf and I knew she was ours, there was a proper way to claim her as a mate and this wasn't it. In the very least, we needed her consent, and a thoroughly satisfying fucking wasn't consent.

I clamped my mouth shut, but stayed over her, making it impossible for her to move as I spurted more cum into her. All the while my wolf snarled, pissed that we hadn't bitten her and marked her for everyone to see.

Soon, I promised him... and myself.

Soon she'd be ours and not because all members of my pack had accepted her, but because, after everything I'd put her through, I'd prove to her that I was a worthy mate and she'd accepted me.

AUDREY

I GASPED FOR BREATH, CAPTURED BENEATH CYRUS'S massive, powerful body, every muscle within me turned to jelly. His cock jerked and more of his heat pumped into me, sending tremors of bliss rushing through me.

That had been—

I had no idea what that had been.

Shocking? Confusing? Amazing?

My soul wept because once again Cyrus and I had sex and I hadn't formed a mating bond with him despite everything within me screaming that he was mine.

The rest of me, however, was a confusing mix of boneless bliss and frustration. I'd seen the look in his wolf-darkened eyes, knew his wolf had taken over, and a mindless primal part of me had instantly submitted. He was the alpha. He was the perfect mate: powerful, strong, and commanding. He was going to fuck me until I couldn't walk and that matching wild primal part of myself *wanted* that. She wanted it so badly that it didn't matter that I still had no idea how he felt about me.

Sure, his wolf wanted to fuck, but that didn't mean he wanted me like my soul wanted him.

I'd sworn to myself that I wouldn't chase after him, but the second he looked at me, I presented like a bitch in heat.

An aftershock of my amazing orgasm rolled through me and my breath caught in my throat. His arms around me tightened and he released a low, purring rumbled, the sound vibrating through my body, relaxing me even more.

Even with everything that had happened between us and with him pressed over top of me, making it impossible for me to move let alone escape, I felt safe. And right now, I ached for that safety. Fighting the grimalkins had been scary, but using my alpha power to make them run away and breathing black smoke had been terrifying.

I didn't know what was happening to me. I'd been fighting to keep my fears away from Knox and Bishop while they were battling the grimalkins and protecting the pack and then from Knox when he was freaking out about me being hurt.

And while I'd tell Bishop and Knox soon, I also hadn't wanted to risk distracting them when their lives were in danger or when they had responsibilities to the pack.

My life wasn't the only one in turmoil right now. Once

again, people had lost loved ones and children had become orphans. There were also the delegates from the alliance to think about and any political fallout that came from the attack, especially if someone important had been hurt or killed — which I really prayed hadn't happened.

Being confused because I wanted Cyrus to prove he cared about me while still letting my primal instincts take over could wait.

I could wait.

It was the responsible thing to do.

"Audrey," he murmured, his gravelly voice shooting heat straight to my core. "I—" He froze and raised his head as if hearing something. "Fuck," he snarled. "I have to go. I—"

He jerked back, his cock sliding out of me and leaving me cold and empty despite the steam filling the shower room.

"Once Molly has wrapped your wounds, have Knox take you to your suite," he said as he stood.

My throat tightened at his hard expression even though I'd already decided that I wasn't the priority right now. His pack was in the middle of an emergency and from his expression, whatever news he'd just gotten was grim.

"I— We need to talk," he said, his tone firm as if he'd made a decision.

And with those ominous words, he stormed out of the shower room.

Swell.

Logically I knew from the past few days that he wasn't the same man who'd yelled at me in the stadium. Even if he was sometimes sharp with me, it didn't feel like it was because of me anymore. It felt more like his anger or frustration or whatever it was that made him close everyone off and demand obedience was because of himself.

Except right now, the stress of the attack and my fears that something was wrong with me, not to mention the fact that he didn't want to talk about it until all the other important things had been taken care of, was making me emotionally sensitive.

Leaving me after fucking me like he was trying to one-up my dream-Knox didn't mean he regretted it or was disgusted by me. It just meant that things were happening and he needed to be the pack's leader, not my lover.

But knowing that and *feeling* that were two different things, and despite wanting to be a strong, independent woman, I felt abandoned... something I couldn't let slip through my mating bond with Knox. He wouldn't understand and would probably try to kill Cyrus the second he saw him.

I stood on still-shaky legs while trying to shove those fears to the back of my mind. I had more important things to worry about, like letting Molly bandage me up then finding Quinn and seeing how Zavier was doing before hurrying out of the hospital to calm Knox down.

And the sooner I did that, the better.

Knox's emotions were roiling, fear and anger and frustration barely contained within him and only partially kept back from flooding our bond. But I could also sense that he was trying to keep it together. He knew I'd needed to go inside and he'd let me go without a fight even though his instincts were telling him to hold me tight and not let go.

I washed off Cyrus's cum and limped out of the shower room. All my aches and pains that Cyrus had momentarily made me forget about flooded back in, and with a groan, I grabbed a towel from the rack just outside the door.

As promised, Molly was waiting for me on the bench around the corner with a med pack, and she quickly got to work bandaging my wounds.

Thankfully, she didn't comment on the fact that Cyrus had just stormed out naked or that the room smelled like sex — because even if I couldn't smell it, I had no doubt it did. And while I was grateful that she didn't say anything, I had no doubt people were going to find out sooner rather than later that I'd had sex with Cyrus.

My insides tightened at the thought of having to deal with more rumors along with the realization that I was alone with the closest of my guys being Knox, who couldn't enter the building.

Sure, I'd killed two grimalkins and scared away two more, but I wouldn't be able to fight members of my new pack like that, not if I wanted to fit in. I already had enough enemies. I needed to make more friends and prove myself worthy.

But first thing first, I had to find people I trusted—

No, I had to check in with Quinn and Zavier. Then I needed to get back to Knox before he completely lost it.

AUDREY

MOLLY TIED THE LAST BANDAGE AND HANDED ME A LOOSE shirt and pants — the pack's version of hospital scrubs. She'd already checked me over with a glowing stone that would indicate if something was wrong with me other than my scrapes and bruises and found no explanation for my queasy stomach.

"Fear, anxiety, and shock," she'd said. "Those grimalkins are terrifying, and Nova said there were three dead ones in Jaxon's smithy. I'm surprised you aren't in deeper shock right now. You should get ahold of me if your symptoms get worse. We're too busy, and we don't have enough beds to keep you here for observation. But you should contact me if your stomach gets worse or you start showing other signs of shock."

She reminded me of the shock symptoms I needed to look out for: increased heart rate, breathing problems, being too cold, dizziness, etcetera. Then she gave me directions to where Quinn might be and I hurried out of the locker room.

As instructed, I turned left and headed down the long hall. Molly was pretty sure Quinn would either be in one of the waiting rooms, or in the room they were going to give to Zavier once his injuries had been treated, and since I had to pass through one of the waiting areas to get to the stairs to the patient rooms, I decided to check there first.

As I hurried, the rumble of many voices grew louder and louder, but I expected that. I was racing out of the staff-only area into the public areas, and the pack was in the middle of a crisis. It made sense that people would gather at the hospital.

What I didn't expect was to round a corner and step into a wide hall packed with people.

Shit.

The waiting area had to be full, with those who couldn't fit gathering in the hall, and I really didn't want to push my way through the crowd and draw everyone's attention. Especially if Quinn wasn't here.

Whoever had attacked me on the first night of the summer festival and had ended up poisoning Bishop was still at large, and I knew there were people in the pack who didn't like me.

"Excuse me," I murmured to the closest person, a young woman holding a sleeping baby.

Every instinct I had screamed to make myself small even though I knew that was from years of being scared and helpless. I didn't have to be small anymore. I should have *never* had to be small even when I'd been powerless.

But I still wanted to be cautious because I had no idea how these people would react to me. Not drawing undue attention to myself was always the safest plan, especially when I wasn't with my mates or friends.

"Alpha!" the woman exclaimed far louder than I'd hoped, making everyone nearby look at me.

"Alpha," another woman said, the title making me cringe. Cyrus was the alpha. Bishop and Knox were as well. I was most certainly *not* a pack alpha.

"Yes, thank you," someone else said.

"Alpha—"

"My babies—"

"My pups—"

"I can't thank you enough—"

Everyone started talking at once and crowded closer. A few of the kids who'd been with Quinn and trapped in the smithy with us pushed through the crowd to stand in front of me. For a moment, warmth swelled around my heart, a whispering shifter connection in my soul with everyone in the hall even though I wasn't touching them, wasn't emotionally close to any of them, and barely knew them.

Then my chest tightened with my old fear that there were too many of them and I'd drawn attention to myself. I wasn't supposed to draw attention.

Knox's emotions heaved inside me and I clamped

down on our mating bond. I couldn't risk him running in here to protect me from his own people.

"I was so scared, alpha," a little boy from Quinn's group said to me as he tugged on my burrowed scrubs to get my attention.

"Me, too, alpha. Me, too," others chimed in.

"You were very brave," I told them, squatting to be at eye level, focusing on them and their worried faces and not the crowd of adults all around us.

"But I cried." The little boy's grip on my scrubs tightened.

"That doesn't mean you weren't brave." My heart broke for him and all the other children who'd experienced today's horrors. No child should ever be terrified or see the horrible things they'd seen. I wanted to hold all of them and protect them. I wanted to figure out how to stop the grimalkin attacks for good.

Except I had no idea if that was even possible. It seemed like grimalkins attacked Stonehaven on a semi-regular basis. More than semi-regularly if my experiences with their attacks were anything to go by. I'd only been in this realm for two months and the grimalkins had already attacked twice.

"Being brave doesn't mean you aren't afraid. I was afraid too, and I wanted to cry," I told them. "It means you do what needs to be done despite being afraid. And I saw you— I saw all of you being brave. You tried to be quiet when we needed to be quiet and you helped Quinn with

Zavier when she needed help. You were all very brave, and I'd be proud to defend the pack with you at my side."

I had no idea where the words were coming from, especially since I wasn't really an alpha, and a part of me cringed that I was saying alpha things. But how I felt didn't matter. What mattered were the children, and I watched pride and self-confidence bloom in the eyes of the little boy who'd confessed to crying.

In fact, all the kids looked more determined, as if me just saying a few words helped them feel safer and more in control of their circumstances.

And while yes, I wanted them to know that it was okay to be afraid and sad and all the other emotions, it felt good to give them something I'd never experienced as a child. The knowledge that an alpha of their pack thought they were good enough.

"Della and Jake," Felix, the engineer I'd met at the summer festival, spoke up. A thick white bandage had been wrapped around his head. "Give Alpha Audrey some space." He stood from one of the few seats against the wall and motioned for me to sit.

I offered him a grateful smile because I was exhausted and my stomach was still queasy. "Thanks, but I need to find Quinn first. Does anyone know where she is?"

"She's waiting for Zavier in his room," an older woman replied, her grim expression souring the satisfaction I felt from consoling the children. That didn't look like Zavier was in good condition. "Take the stairs at the end of the hall and go to the second floor. She'll be some-where on that main hall."

She pointed in the direction I'd originally been going, indicating I needed to push through the entire crowd.

"Thank you." I straightened from my crouch and pushed through the people, a strange mix of pride, happiness, and embarrassment churning in my stomach.

All of these people looked at me like I was someone. For the first time I was being seen. I had value and respect, and people cared about me. But on the other hand, people were *looking* at me and my lifetime of trying to be invisible made me uncomfortable with being the center of attention.

More people thanked me, some regarded me with awe, others with respect, and I tried to keep my head high while quietly acknowledging their thanks and comments.

The crowd parted to let me pass, and I kept my pace even as I walked to the stairs, even as the churning in my stomach grew stronger.

I didn't know how to behave. All I knew was that fleeing would make me look like prey and I was done with being prey. That, and an alpha didn't flee. And if everyone was calling me alpha, I had to live up to the role whether I wanted to be one or not.

AUDREY

I found Quinn in the sixth patient room on the right, sitting in a chair beside the bed and holding Zavier's paw. His fur had been shaved from most of his body and large white bandages encircled his torso as well as three of his four legs. His eyes were closed and his breath came in short sharp pants, indicating that even while unconscious, he was in pain.

"Audrey," Quinn cried when she saw me, and she sprang up and rushed the few feet to me, wrapping me in a tight embrace. "Thank the Sisters you're all right."

"Thank the Sisters *you're* all right," I replied, hugging her back.

I'd been terrified for Quinn and the children during that fight, and it was such a relief to see she only had one bandage around her forearm and no other injuries.

Zavier whimpered, drawing her attention, and worry squeezed around my heart. He didn't look good, and

Quinn looked wrecked. Even if I was wrong and there wasn't anything more than sisterly affection for her adoptive brother, the two of them were still close, and it would destroy her if he died.

"You were amazing, you know," Quinn said, her voice soft, her gaze locked on Zavier. "Thanks to you none of the children were hurt. Not even a scratch."

I tightened my grip around her, hoping physical contact with me would help steady her soul even as I selfishly used my shifter connection with her to steady mine.

My insides squirmed with the need to help her, help those children. Help my pack.

"So what happens next?" I asked even though I was sore and exhausted.

There were people hurt worse than me and just as tired, and I was sure they were doing their duty.

"After all the grimalkins are dead and the injured are taken care of?"

I nodded.

She swallowed hard. "After that come the funerals."

My throat tightened as if I could feel her grief and fear. Her parents had died when she was young, probably because of a grimalkin attack or something just as horrible, and now there was a chance the not-brother she loved was going to die too.

"Then we rebuild and—" Quinn said as Nova stepped into the doorway of the hospital room and gave me a stern look.

"You're supposed to be resting and letting the elixir do

its thing," Nova said. "Go. Rest. The pack is still hosting a formal dinner for the alliance members tonight, and Cyrus and Bishop will want you there."

"They're still going to hold it?" I asked even though this was my first time hearing about it, although I was sure Bishop would have mentioned it once the town tour for the delegates and their aides was over.

"More than half of the work is already done," Nova said.

"Yeah, Eloise and Kira have been working on the dinner for over a week now," Quinn added.

"But a lot of the alliance members stayed to fight," I insisted. "Some of them will be hurt." Or dead, but I didn't want to say that out loud.

"Everyone still needs to eat." Nova's expression turned grim. "They'll also want to discuss what happened, possibly blame Cyrus and Bishop for not providing enough protection. Having a meal while they talk about it will partially distract them. Hopefully, that will help them keep an honest perspective on this. We've lost far too many people in the last few months to grimalkin attacks."

And while a part of me wanted to argue with Nova and say I could help, the rest of me was exhausted and worried. Somehow, I'd controlled those grimalkins and threw up black smoke. Getting to the bottom of that was as important as helping out, possibly more so.

For all I knew, I was dangerous. Sterling had already

influenced me into hurting myself. What if the smoke was connected to him... what if the grimalkins were?

He'd been able to control those shadow snake monsters through the rip between my old realm and this one. What if he could somehow control the grimalkins? Their alpha power felt a little like the heavy ominous power in Anakar, and that power came from Tzanagoth.

I was probably grasping at straws, searching for an explanation for something that had no explanation. Grimalkins were mindless beasts. They attacked because they attacked not because of some evil magic seeping from the ground.

Except I couldn't make myself believe that. Even animals in my realm had reasons for attacking an obviously more powerful pack. Sure, the grimalkins could take a single shifter one on one, but not the whole pack. Something had to have made them think this attack, and the one that had happened when I'd first gotten here, was a good idea or at least the better of two terrible options.

"Go," Nova insisted, a whisper of her power rolling over me, not enough to make me submit but enough to tell me she was serious. "You need your rest."

Nova directed me to stairs at the back of the hospital so I could leave the building without being swarmed again, and I hurried outside to reunite with Knox before he lost control of his wolf— or rather lost control of the primal wildness at the core of his wolf's soul.

"Nova says there's nothing wrong with you," Knox said as he yanked me close and held me as if I was the only thing keeping him in his human form, which I probably was.

Given how much stress leaked through our mating bond, I was surprised he hadn't shifted into his wolf.

"I still feel like I've gone ten rounds with a grimalkin," I replied, sinking into his embrace and savoring the heat of our shifter connection warming around my heart.

"Then you're not going to the formal dinner tonight." Knox swept me into his arms so he cradled me against his chest and headed up a deserted narrow street toward the Residence, completely naked.

"I have to," I said, pressing my nose into the hollow at the base of his throat and breathing in his rich wood smoke scent.

I also *wanted* to go. If I was there, I might notice or overhear something important. And despite the positive reception I'd just received in the hospital, I still needed to feel useful, still needed to prove my worth to this pack.

Besides, I had an ability no one else had. I could understand every language in this realm because of the magic in the rip between this realm and mine, not just the one spoken by the pack. I was the only one who could fully observe the Mountain and Sea Alliance delegates and their aides and, more importantly, the merchants.

I hadn't seen the merchants or their powerful monster-killing weapons after the grimalkins attacked. All I knew was that none of them had fled with the aides and translators who couldn't fight, and a part of me screamed that I needed to find them and find out what they were up to.

Because they were up to something.

It had been chaos when the grimalkins attacked, but if I thought back to that first moment, only one of the three merchants had looked surprised. The other two had worn strangely blank expressions as if they were trying to hide what they were feeling.

Of course, Cyrus, Representative Folmar, and King Gower hadn't looked surprised, either. They'd all looked angry. But they'd at least had an expression.

Knox growled, the sound rumbling in his chest. "I don't want you to go." Then he huffed. "I don't want to go, either."

"To the dinner?" I asked, surprised. There was no way Cyrus would demand Knox go inside the Residence and be surrounded by anyone, let alone all of the delegates and aides. That was the fastest way to get him to snap and Cyrus knew that.

"No," he snarled. "I don't want you to go to the dinner, and I don't want to leave you for a hunt."

He blew out a heavy breath then pressed his nose to the top of my head and inhaled my scent.

"We have to send hunters— hell, send anyone still able to fight to scour the area around town for more grimalkins," he said. "Deacon's only given me enough time to ensure you get back to your suite. Then I have to go."

My heart stuttered with a ridiculous fear for him and

for how long he might be gone. It was silly. Hunting was his job in the pack, and he needed to make sure there weren't more grimalkins out there waiting to attack.

I knew of at least two grimalkins that were still alive and had no idea how long they'd obey my command... if I'd actually commanded them.

No, I *had* commanded them. And as much as I wanted to crawl into bed and nurse my aches and pains until the formal dinner, I needed to talk to Whil and find out what was wrong with me... or possibly right. Controlling the grimalkins may have made me sick, but it had saved everyone in the smithy.

Knox carried me down the narrow streets and alleys, avoiding the main roads and anyone who might be on them. He hurried along the winding Old Town streets and through the open main gate of the Residence.

It had been eerily quiet after we'd gotten a few blocks from the hospital and even farther away from the market and the chaos, and it was still quiet on the Residence's grounds despite that the Residence would be hosting a diplomatic dinner in four or five hours.

I still couldn't believe Cyrus was going through with the dinner, despite Nova's perfectly logical explanation.

Knox rounded the side of the large castle complete with multiple wings and turrets to the French doors leading into my suite.

"I want to stay," he said, his voice low as he slowly lowered me, letting me slide down his naked body.

Worry and yearning and anger radiated through our

bond, and I pushed as much love and confidence back to him as I could.

"I'll be fine. I'll have Bishop whenever he's done with whatever he's doing." Although whatever that was, it was upsetting him. He'd almost completely blocked his emotions from me and what little that was seeping through our mating bond was anger and grief. "You need to protect our pack."

"Our pack?" he asked, his pride swelling into me despite his expression remaining hard.

"Yes, our pack," I repeated.

I'd thought the pack was mine when I'd been defending, Quinn, Zavier, and the pups in the smithy, and I felt it even more now. Whether I was actually an alpha or not, this pack and these people were mine.

"Alpha." Knox tangled his fingers in my hair, drew my head back, and captured my lips in a searing kiss.

It wasn't as wild as his usual kisses, I could tell he was trying to be mindful of my injuries, but it burned with passion and need. It claimed me as his, always his, and I happily submitted to him.

Deep in my soul, I knew I was safe with Knox. We might have had a rocky, unwanted start, but love and commitment roared through our mating bond. He'd do whatever it took to protect me and love me, and I loved him for that. I especially loved that the emotions in our bond didn't feel insincere, like they were all his and the mating bond wasn't compelling him to love me. He'd more than made his peace with being mate bonded with me, and he loved it. He loved me.

With a groan, he jerked away and shifted into his massive black wolf, his head reaching to the middle of my chest.

Must go, he growled in my head before bounding away and leaving me with my breath a little too fast, a warm ache in my core, and my lips tingling for more.

Love you, I thought at him even though I didn't have telepathy. I still needed to tell him. *Stay safe.*

AUDREY

I WAITED FOR A FEW SECONDS ON MY SUITE'S PATIO TO make sure Knox had a good head start and would hopefully be off the Residence's grounds by the time I walked around the front of the castle.

If he saw me, he'd insist I go to bed, and if I told him about the black smoke and controlling the grimalkins, he'd freak out. And that wouldn't be helpful at the moment. Searching the area around Stonehaven and ensuring everyone in the pack was safe, not just me, was important. Without a doubt, he was the most powerful hunter they had, and they needed him. I didn't want to get in the way of that.

And while I didn't want to hide anything from him, I also couldn't distract him from his duties. Once I'd talked to Whil, I'd have a better idea what was going on and I'd tell Bishop. It was a bit of a cop out, but Bishop wouldn't freak out and he'd know how to talk with Knox to keep him from losing it.

With that decided, I summoned my strength, pushing through my exhaustion and aches and went to Whil's greenhouse library cottage. The building was tucked against a large protective wall at the back of the grounds. Bushes and trees and vines were all in full bloom regardless that it was summer and some of the plants bloomed in the spring or fall. They crowded around the half English cottage half greenhouse structure giving it a whimsical, magical feel, which was fitting for the home of a summer fae.

I knocked on the wooden doorframe to the greenhouse. "Whil?"

No answer.

"Whil?" I tried again as I took a few steps inside.

Still no answer.

Maybe she was in the cottage half of the building.

I headed deeper into the greenhouse, walking through a garden bursting with brilliant flowers and vibrant leaves. Bookshelves crammed with books and scrolls and knickknacks hid amongst the greenery, growing more predominant the farther I walked.

I followed a path that was half wide flagstone and half moss or short grass, and up a step or two, then back down again, or down then back up with no noticeable reason for the steps, until I reached the seating area at the back made up of mismatching pieces of furniture. Beyond the sitting area stood an archway heading into the cottage proper.

"Whil?"

But before I'd even spoken, I knew she wasn't home, or if she was, she was sleeping or concentrating on something. The cottage and greenhouse felt too still, too empty.

Of course, now that I thought about it, it made sense that she wasn't home. She might not have been a shifter, but she was still a member of the pack and even with her minimal sorcerer's ability, she could still help.

Swell. I'd have to wait to get answers and I'd walked to the back of the Residence's grounds for nothing.

With a sigh, I marched back to my suite and collapsed on my bed.

Loud knocking and someone calling my name woke me, and for a second, I couldn't remember where I was.

Then it all came flooding back. I was in a realm with two moons and dangerous beasts. The son of my previous pack's alpha and his friend had tricked me into starting a mating bond and then tried to sacrifice me to a monster. I was mate bonded with two of three pack alphas — and wanted to be mated to the third as well — and now I was breathing smoke and controlling grimalkins.

"Audrey," Quinn called, her voice muffled with my door and my suite's sitting room between us.

"Coming," I called back, realizing I hadn't undressed out of my borrowed scrubs or even crawled under the blankets. I'd just collapsed on top of my bed.

I hurried out of my bedroom, surprised that I wasn't as sore and achy as I would have expected after the fight. I rushed across the lavish sitting room with its handcrafted everything, unlocked the door, and opened it.

"What are you doing here?" I asked. "You should be with Zavier."

Quinn offered me a weak smile and held up a garment bag and a handbag as if that explained everything. "Whil put him into a magical sleep so he can heal without pain, and I'd already promised Bishop I'd help you get ready for tonight."

"I'm sure Bishop would understand if you wanted to stay with Zavier," I told her even as I stepped back to let her in.

"Zavier won't wake until tomorrow and I couldn't keep sitting there and crying. I *know* he'll recover. It's just going to take a while." Her weak smile turned into a fierce one that looked anything but happy. "It could be worse. Last I heard, twenty pack members had died and two dozen were injured like Zavier."

I swallowed hard, the wildness rising within me at the thought that I'd lost twenty shifters and even more were hurt. They were mine to protect and I'd failed them. Even if I couldn't have been there to help them, I'd still failed them somehow.

"Five humans, two gryphons, and three Dedearc died as well," Quinn continued as she walked through my sitting room and bedroom and into the bathroom. "More were hurt, but Representative Folmar's son is the worst."

"Cohnal?" I asked, relief sweeping through me. He might be hurt, but from how Quinn mentioned him, it meant he was still alive after fighting three grimalkins by himself.

"He lost half of his leg, was blinded in one eye, and I'm told his beautiful feathers were shredded. Sit here," Quinn said, pointing to the edge of the tub. "Let's see how many scrapes and bruises I have to cover up."

I huffed and sat. "I wouldn't bother trying. You'd have to wrap me in a full bodysuit with a mask to cover up the fact that I went toe to toe against a grimalkin."

Although it could have been worse. Poor Cohnal had lost his leg, and his feathers had been damaged. I didn't know if they'd grow back because I knew nothing about gryphons. Up until this morning, I thought gryphon shifters were only a myth.

"You mean *many* grimalkins, not *a* grimalkin," Quinn said her expression daring me to argue with her. "You killed two grimalkins without shifting, and your alpha power..." She barked a harsh laugh and started pulling jars and bottles and tubes from her bag. "I don't think Finn even knew what he was doing until he killed that grimalkin. You must be amazing at blocking your power because it feels like you don't have any."

"Right now, I don't," I confessed. "It only shows up when I'm upset and that only started happening recently."

Quinn frowned at me so I told her about my pack and how my ancestors had cursed themselves and future generations so we could hide among the humans. I also told her how the curse was broken on the summer solstice after our eighteenth birthday, how mine was still in place, and how now it didn't matter if we were shifters or not. The archangel Michael had proclaimed war on all humans and every supernatural being had stepped up to save them.

Quinn did my makeup while listening, and I went on to tell her about Sterling and Royce betraying me and me hopefully fucking up his plans by still being alive.

"I'm glad your pack doesn't have to hide anymore, but I can't believe someone tried to exterminate a whole realm," she said, motioning for me to turn around.

"Some people are like that. Greedy, hungry for power," I said, obeying her and turning. "They'll crush anyone who's weaker than them to get what they want."

"There's something wrong with them if that's the way they are," she huffed as she gathered strands of my hair, twisting and braiding them into a complicated updo that only required six simple pins to keep it in place.

After she was done, we returned to my bedroom and she unzipped the garment bag. The dress inside was similar in design to the one I'd worn this morning with a thin neck strap and a higher back, except this one was gold with delicate green embroidery.

"Where's Bishop getting these dresses?" I asked. "They fit perfectly and hide half the scars on my back."

"He ordered a bunch of them specially made for you

just before the festival," Quinn said. "And he's got great taste. You look amazing."

Quinn turned me so I could see myself in the two-person wide full-length mirror. My breath caught in my throat. Somehow, she'd made me beautiful.

The makeup was soft and subtle, just enough to highlight my eyes and hide the worst of the cuts and bruises, and my hair was twisted and curled with tendrils framing my face and accentuating my neck. The dress clung to my barely-there curves, but still seemed to cover the fact that I hadn't gained back all the weight I'd lost during my heat fever and even my bruises and cuts — those that could be seen — seemed paler, as if they were a few days old instead of a few hours. Molly must have given me an elixir from a particularly potent batch.

"Your alphas won't be able to keep their eyes off you," Quinn said.

At her words, the memory of Cyrus kissing me like he wanted to claim me, his eyes hungry and dark with his wolf, shuddered through me.

Not my alpha.

And once we had our *talk,* I was sure he was going to make that clear.

Except my stupid soul didn't want to listen to reason. He was mine, just like Bishop and Knox.

AUDREY

Quinn packed up her beauty supplies looking exhausted and emotionally raw. Doing my hair and makeup had been a slight reprieve from her worries, but only that. They weren't going to go away until she knew Zavier had pulled through.

"You'll have to tell me about the party tomorrow," she said with a weak smile. "To distract me."

"I will," I promised. "Are you going home to rest?"

"I'm going to try," she replied, but she was probably going to toss and turn for a few hours then go to the hospital and try to sleep in the chair beside Zavier's bed. "Bishop said he has to schmooze and couldn't escort you, but he promised he'll stick by your side the entire night."

That was a relief.

Although I still wasn't sure how I was going to handle being in a room full of powerful people and not give in to my urges to shrink in on myself or find a way to slip away.

Quinn left and I sucked in a deep breath to steady my nerves. Bishop and Knox loved me and Bishop believed in me. That, and I'd just killed two grimalkins. I could face the dignitaries and aides.

They at least, wouldn't be trying to rip me to pieces.

With my back straight and my head held high, I marched down the halls inside the Residence to the grand front entrance and the main doors to the ballroom.

Standing at the threshold between the hall and grand entrance, I couldn't see into the ballroom, but I could hear the voices of people as well as soft music coming from inside. Before me, tiny rainbows shimmered on the thick, red rug, reflections of the bright lights in the crystal chandelier, and the grand staircase framed the doors to the ballroom. It started split at the bottom, curled up to a landing, creating a balcony, before splitting again to rise to the next floor.

But my gaze stalled on the landing and didn't follow the curving stairs all the way to the top.

Finn, looking tired and pale from his battle with the grimalkins, stood at the top of the stairs staring at me.

I squared my shoulders. He and Velora were the two betas who'd accused me of seducing both Knox and Bishop to gain the power and privilege of being a pack alpha, and I'd essentially taken control of his body with my alpha power, something that probably pissed him off even more.

Well, fine.

Finn could yell at me all he liked for using my alpha

power on him when he was a beta and I wasn't really an alpha, but I refused to feel bad or even guilty. I'd done what needed to be done to save those children and everyone else in the smithy, and just like how I'd stood up against Cyrus for saving those children after the first grimalkin attack, I'd stand my ground against Finn now.

What I didn't want was to be reamed out in front of the doorway to the ballroom where all the dignitaries and aides could see me.

I pulled my attention away from him, about to hurry inside. After the day I'd had, I didn't want to have to deal with his or Velora's shit. Surely Finn wouldn't want to make a scene in front of everyone.

Except he called out my name and hurried down the stairs.

Shit. Did I rush to find Bishop? He'd said he'd meet me in the ballroom. Or did I look for some place more private?

But the thought of being alone with the big beta made my insides churn. It didn't matter that I'd been able to control him with my alpha power. My power wasn't predictable. I might not be able to summon it to protect myself since all the times it had manifested was in defense of someone else.

I also wanted witnesses. In my old pack, it wouldn't have mattered if someone watched one of the betas yell at me, but here it did. Here, I had people willing to stand up for me and protect me.

I strode toward the ballroom.

"Audrey, wait." Finn's power snapped over me but wasn't enough to stop me. "Alpha," he added as he leaped over the railing eight steps from the floor to land in front of me.

"Beta," I replied, uncertain if he'd called me alpha or someone in the doorway who I now couldn't see because of his broad frame.

"Alpha, please." He dropped to his knees in front of me and lifted his chin while tilting his head, baring his throat in full submission to me. To. Me. The weakest shifter—

No. Not anymore. My power might only come out when I needed to protect someone, but I wasn't weak. Not anymore.

Behind him, the people in the doorway noticed, and a hush fell over the ballroom. My stomach churned with all the attention but I held my ground. If I wanted to win over those reluctant to accept me as an alpha, I needed to act like one.

"I beg you, alpha, forgive me. I was wrong to suspect you were anything other than a gift from the Sisters to our pack," he said as he clasped his hands behind his back. "I treated you unfairly and am ashamed to confess I didn't keep my feelings about you to myself. You shouldn't have had to prove yourself to me, and I didn't deserve your kindness when you saved me."

I didn't think I'd been particularly kind to Finn during the fight with the grimalkins. I'd needed his help and had forced him into action, but I also wasn't going to argue with him.

"I failed as a beta and the Watch Commander," he continued. "I can recommend a few good men and women who can replace me. I only beg you let me remain in the pack."

Replace him? Remain in the pack?

What the hell?

I wasn't going to kick him out or try to convince Bishop and Cyrus to replace him. It wasn't my place to make that kind of decision... or was it?

I was pretty sure calling me alpha was a courtesy because I was mated to Knox and Bishop. I didn't want the responsibility of leading the pack—

Except I did want to protect it. I wanted everyone to know their loved ones would come home at night, and I really wanted every child to feel safe and loved.

Did that mean I wanted to be alpha?

Knox and Bishop were already my mates and a part of my soul was certain Cyrus was too — despite us having sex three times now and still not forming a mating bond like I had with my other mates.

"Finn," I said softly, my instincts screaming to stop drawing attention to myself because that had been my reality all my life until a few months ago. "A suspicious Watch Commander isn't a bad thing. I won't asked Bishop or Cyrus to replace you. But you also need to realize that kindness and understanding are not weaknesses. You should have tried to get to know me before making up your mind."

He frowned. "I asked you questions."

"You interrogated me and made accusations."

He dipped his head forward, his expression contrite.

"Yes, I didn't want to tell you about my origins. I was afraid," I continued. "If you'd shown me kindness, I would have opened up more like I did with Bishop."

I probably still would have been hesitant and he would have needed patience, but I'd become more comfortable with Nova, Deacon, Eloise, and Kira and they'd easily seen that I was scared and lonely.

"You also didn't take into consideration your alphas' opinions about me before making up your mind," I added.

"I promise, I'll do better," he replied, his volume just as low as mine.

"I know you will." I offered him a soft smile. It was still going to take a while for me to trust him, but I didn't like the idea of him being afraid of me. I wanted allies not enemies.

Cyrus strode out of the ballroom and placed a hand on Finn's shoulder.

"Beta," he said, his gaze locked with mine, his expression soft and strange until I realized he'd heard our conversation with his enhanced shifter hearing. Then the strange expression sort of looked like pride? "Time to get back to work."

"He's still recovering," I blurted out.

But Cyrus didn't snap back at me. There wasn't even a flicker of his power indicating I'd upset him. Instead, the probably-pride shifted to something else, something strange and hard.

"No, the alpha is right," Finn told me. "Deacon and I haven't fully confirmed all the grimalkins are dead."

Finn ducked his head and hurried back up the stairs.

I turned my attention to Cyrus. "He looked tired and pale."

"He's not doing any hunting, just coordinating," Cyrus replied. "He'll be fine. Everyone who can needs to step up."

He raked his gaze down my body, and a flash of dark hunger filled his eyes before the hardness returned.

So, he craved me, but was going to tell me it could only be sex. That was what he wanted to talk about.

I raised my chin and swallowed back my disappointment, even as my insides heated at the memory of him pounding into me.

"You have a job to do, too," he said with a pointed look, his voice gruff. "Come on."

Right. Eavesdropping on the merchants and other members of the alliance.

Cyrus stepped aside, gestured for me to enter the completely quiet ballroom, and my heart pounded. Everyone stared at me and it took everything I had not to shrink in on myself.

It's not like my old pack. They aren't staring, waiting for me to be humiliated—

Although from Velora's barely veiled death glare, I was sure *she* was waiting for the right moment.

She hadn't been happy when Bishop had told her we were mated, and she was furious when she realized I had two mating marks. That proved Bishop and I hadn't just mated with promises. We'd actually completed the rare, sacred vows and sealed our bond with a bite.

And it didn't matter that neither of us had said the vows to create the magical bond between us. She didn't need to know that.

Especially since she wouldn't recognize that we were fated mates like almost everyone else did. She'd argued that I'd manipulated Knox and she'd argue again that I manipulated Bishop in the same way.

I heaved my attention from Velora, knowing I needed to ignore her and be brave... and, if I was smart, remember to keep my guard up.

BISHOP

Every time I looked at Audrey, she stole my breath. I'd arrived in the ballroom a few moments ago, expecting to find her already here and had been worried when I hadn't seen her. But her entry now made that momentary burst of fear that her injuries were worse than expected worth it.

She was a goddess stepping through the open double doors into the brightly lit room. Her makeup was delicately done, hiding all but the shadows of the scrapes and bruises on her face, accentuating her beauty but not erasing the proof of her courage, and her hair twisted over her head in a stunning, complicated style. Flecks of shimmering gold caught the light in her blond strands, adding to her divine etherealness, and the golden dress I'd had made just for her clung perfectly to her scant curves — curves I intended to grow with good food, peace, and love.

My mate would never have to fear for her life — at least once we'd dealt with the grimalkins and caught whoever or *whatever* had tried to kill her — and she'd never wonder when she'd get her next meal.

She was flourishing before my eyes, bravely facing everyone in the room with her head held high and not afraid to make eye contact. That never would have happened when she'd first arrived. Hell, she'd been looking at the ground and shrinking into herself two weeks ago.

She was still nervous — I could feel it crackling through our mating bond — but she didn't look it. I could even feel a hint of her alpha power softly rolling off her as if after standing her ground against Cyrus to go to the healing pools and fighting with the grimalkins, it hadn't fully retreated back behind her curse.

Knox had mentioned the same thing when he'd told me she was okay and that I had to keep watch over her while he hunted. But whether the curse was crumbling or not, it didn't matter. I fell in love with her when she didn't have a speck of power. If her alpha power never manifested again, I'd still love her.

Although it did feel as if things were changing for her. Just like she was breaking through her fears and claiming her place and her worth in this pack, her alpha power was breaking through her curse.

Soon everyone would be able to see what I saw, that she belonged at my and my brothers' sides.

And while I knew Cyrus was still fighting with

himself because he thought our pack wouldn't accept her, his body language, the fact that he stood too close to her, told me he'd accepted the truth— or rather, his wolf had fully embraced the truth. Audrey was his mate.

Now all I needed was for his human half to catch up and stop making life confusing and stressful for Audrey.

I loved my brother, but his need to control everything while also sacrificing himself to the pack made me want to strangle him. He deserved to be happy, too. Hell, he'd probably be a better alpha to our pack if he was happy.

He, however, wasn't going to change overnight. I needed to be patient and wait for the right moment to give him that final push to tell Audrey how he feels.

I just hoped to the Sisters that it would come soon. The sexual tension between them was driving me crazy.

Plastering a pleasant smile on my face, I slipped through the crowd, and joined them just as they reached Jundar.

"Audrey, this is Speaker Jundar, General of the Ciliran forces," Cyrus said. "Speaker, this is my brothers' mate, Audrey."

Jundar, a stocky man with white short-cropped hair that stood out sharply from his dark skin, smiled at Audrey even before Yara, a small woman with large dark eyes and long wild hair, had finished translating Cyrus's words in to Cilirinian, not because he understood our language, but that it was clear Cyrus was making introductions.

Jundar's smile deepened as he bowed his head and said something back.

Audrey waited for Yara to translate, a blush already forming on her cheeks, though I doubted anyone but me and maybe Cyrus noticed.

Then she opened her mouth, looked at Jundar instead of the translator as was proper, and said two short words in Cilirinian.

Both Jundar's and Yara's eyes widened in surprise. A glower flickered over Cyrus's expression before he schooled it back to something still hard but more pleasant while my pulse lurched.

I hadn't wanted to reveal Audrey's ability to understand every language in this realm and not just because it let her listen in on conversations we couldn't understand. Our allies would ask questions that I didn't want Audrey to have to answer, not until she felt more secure in this realm and our pack.

Jundar said something, and panic snapped through our mating bond.

Thankfully, Audrey's expression remained neutral before shortly slipping into a frown when Yara didn't automatically speak, pretending she hadn't understood Jundar.

Yara glanced at Jundar, who gave a slight nod, telling her to translate.

"The speaker didn't realize you could speak Cilirinian," Yara said.

Audrey opened her mouth then snapped it shut, her gaze jumping to mine.

"She's only learned a few niceties," I replied for her as I joined their group while praying Audrey had only said thank you or something similar in Cilirinian. "She's far from fluent."

"Too bad," Yara translated. "I like Yara—" A smile pulled at Yara's lips. "But speaking through her still makes for an awkward conversation."

"Maybe next time the Alliance meets Audrey will know more." I tugged Audrey closer to my side and nuzzled the top of her head to breathe in her scent. "Will you excuse us? I haven't talked to my mate all day."

Jundar and Yara gave us knowing smiles, and I drew Audrey away from them to our table. No one else was near, they were all gathered on the dance floor talking and waiting for dinner to officially start.

"Thanks for that," Audrey said as I pulled out a chair for her. "I hadn't even realized I'd spoken in Cilirinian until I saw their expressions."

She sat and I sat beside her, my wolf urging me to move our chairs closer together. "I kind of got that from the panic rushing through our bond."

"But you covered for me perfectly and set me up to be able to speak Cilirinian the next time we see the speaker," she said.

"It's your decision when or if you want anyone to know about your fluency in languages." I brushed my lips against hers, savoring their softness as well as the love billowing through our bond. "I'll always have your back."

"I know you will." She leaned closer and deepened our kiss, filling it with a promise of something more later tonight.

Which was good. Knox and I had plans for her, and while I needed to remember to be gentle because of her injuries from the fight, I wasn't going to be able to keep my hands off her. Our bond was still so new and we'd finally gotten back from the healing pools to some privacy.

"Ah, the newly mated," Deacon laughed, his voice right in my ear.

Audrey jerked back, her face a brilliant red, which only made Deacon laugh harder.

"Sorry, alphas," he said, "but you've drawn a bit of an audience."

Horror seeped through our bond as she glanced at the dance floor from where almost everyone stared at us.

"Something joyous to celebrate in the middle of such heartache," Folmar said. "To the newly mated alphas! May you be blessed with many healthy cubs."

The rest of the room joined her toast, and Audrey's blush rushed down her neck and spread, her darkened skin highlighting the shimmering twined bond marks on the side of her throat. A throat I couldn't wait to bite again.

Sisters, I couldn't wait to get her alone.

AUDREY

I SAT THROUGH DINNER SMILING AND NODDING AND LETTING Bishop answer any direct comments to me from anyone who used a translator for fear of speaking in a language I wasn't supposed to know. Again.

God, I couldn't believe I'd done that, but it made sense. My brain thought everyone was speaking English regardless of what language they were really speaking.

I also couldn't believe I'd forgotten I was in a room full of people and kissed Bishop like I wanted to have sex with him... which I did, but now wasn't the place or time.

It was like I'd lost my mind or something. I'd experienced a little bit of power, and I'd forgotten everything that had been beaten and scolded into me.

Except it wasn't my alpha power and killing those grimalkins that made me more confident. It was everyone else. Bishop and Knox's love, the uncomfortable praise

I'd gotten from the people in the hospital, and even Finn recognizing I just wanted to belong with the pack.

Sure, there were still lots of people who look down on me, but now I knew their opinion, just like Merrick's, Sterling's, and Royce's, didn't matter. That and it was almost impossible to keep my hands to myself.

Bishop and I were newly mated, and the urge to drag him out of the ballroom and lock ourselves in my suite was almost overwhelming. We'd had sex to seal our bond and again the next morning after we'd saved him, and that had been it since our time at the healing pools. Over a week with my mate and only a few teasing touches and kisses because I really didn't want to embarrass myself in front of Deacon, Whil, and...

A shiver of desire rushed through me along with a flashback of me and Cyrus in the shower room.

Yeah, I wanted Cyrus to watch me having sex with Bishop and Knox, wanted to see a possessive heat burn in his eyes.

Except I had a feeling that was never going to happen. He'd said we needed to talk and that was never a good sign.

I'd thought we were building something. I'd felt the way he'd looked at me during our march back to Stonehaven from the healing pools. Even more telling, he'd made an effort to be nice to me, encouraging me and asking instead of commanding.

But he had serious responsibilities being the primary

alpha of the pack, and I had no doubt he couldn't take a mate just because he wanted to.

The thought turned the wine in my mouth sour, and I swallowed it down against the lump forming in my throat.

Damn it. I was used to disappointment. It shouldn't bother me that Cyrus might desire me, might want to have sex with me, but didn't want to mate with me.

Except my soul was certain he was my mate and it hurt thinking that he was going to reject me.

"Wow," Bishop said as he leaned close. "That was one hell of a mood swing. Don't worry, the dinner is almost done."

His warm breath caressed my cheek and teased down my neck. Desire blossomed within me and I struggled to think of chilling thoughts before I blasted the room with my arousal and a third of everyone in attendance knew I wanted to jump Bishop.

He hummed, the sound a low rumbled, and smiled. "That's better."

For him, maybe, but not for me. Now I couldn't stop thinking about dragging Bishop back to my room and having my way with him.

The dessert dishes were cleared away and then the speeches began. Cyrus welcomed the delegates and their aides to Stonehaven and spoke the grief everyone felt, since every delegation had lost someone. The other leaders each stood and thanked Cyrus for the welcome as well as acknowledging our pack's grief.

After King Gower, who was a charismatic speaker, I tuned out the other leaders and let my gaze wander, trying to not stare at the merchants for too long. One of the merchants had the strange, flat expression that I'd seen just before the grimalkins had attacked, making me think he was trying to hide his reaction, the other two looked serious.

Except, even with the serious expressions, it felt like they were anticipating something. Which made sense. After this morning's tragedy as well as the evidence of the effectiveness of their weapons, they had to feel certain the alliance would agree to buy their lightning guns.

The whole situation was a very convenient coincidence for the merchants, and while I doubted they were responsible for bringing the grimalkins to Stonehaven, something still felt off about them.

After the speeches, Eloise and Kira set up evening sweets and drinks on a long table at the side of the room, and the musicians — the group who'd been playing at the summer festival — started playing dance music. These dances were still choreographed numbers where everyone knew the movement, but they were slower, more stately, than the ones at the festival.

Bishop grabbed my hands and I stiffened. I didn't want to embarrass him or Cyrus in front of everything, and I would if I stepped onto the dance floor.

"Don't worry," he murmured against my cheek, sending a shiver racing down my spine. "I've got something better planned than dancing."

"Something more private?" I breathed, as his desire swelled through our mating bond and enflamed mine.

We slipped out the door to the kitchen to avoid notice, hurried past Eloise and Kira and the dozens of other people who were helping with the party, and raced out into the herb garden.

Bishop's grip on my hand tightened. "This way."

We rushed around the back of the Residence then headed deeper into the garden, away from the building. The second I saw the hedgerow in the distance, I knew where we were going.

The summer garden.

We'd had our first date there and instead of eating the picnic we'd made love. It seemed every time we went to the summer garden, we forgot why we'd gone there and ended up having sex.

And from the anticipation and need rushing through our bond, we were going to make love again.

Feeling freer than I'd ever felt in my life, I ran with Bishop through the winter garden and stepped through the wrought iron arch between the gardens into magic.

The summer garden had been transformed into a nighttime wonderland. Night-blooming flowers that had secretly been hidden among all the glorious daytime blooms shimmered pale white, blue, and pink in patches through the whole area, and a night-blooming vine twisted among the clematises, honeysuckle, and wisteria, climbing up and over the top of the pergola in the garden's center.

Soft light emanated from trays of little white stones inside the pergola, and in the center were dozens of pillows all white with gold trim and a soft-looking dark blue blanket.

"It's beautiful," I breathed.

I couldn't believe Bishop had done this for me or where he might have found the time to set it up with everything he'd had to do in the aftermath of the grimalkin attack.

"*You're* beautiful," he said as he stepped close behind me and teased his lips along my jaw.

With a sigh, I tipped my head back, resting it against his chest, and sank into the warmth, love, and desire rolling through our mating bond.

"Just because we're mated now doesn't mean I'm going to stop courting you," he murmured in my ear, his hot breath sending need racing straight to my core. "I promise to show you every day how beautiful you are and how much I love you."

His fingers brushed down my bare arms, drawing another blast of need, adding to the heat building between my thighs. I ached for him like I always ached for him.

He was my first love, my first real kiss, the first man to be kind to me, my first... my first everything, and I knew I wasn't in love with him because he was kind to me when everyone else had been cruel. I was in love with him because he filled my soul with certainty and comfort. He was my confidence and passion.

He was home.

He'd always been my home. I'd just needed to run through a rip in the realms to find him.

A large black wolf strode out of the shadows to stand in the middle of the blanket and pillows in the pergola. White light shimmered in his thick coat while lust and pride swelled in my mating bonds.

Knox.

My ferocious, wild mate. He was my courage and fierceness. When we made love, I felt powerful. Despite his need for submission, now that he'd fully committed to our bonding, I never felt lesser or weaker with him. I felt like an equal.

A hint of alpha power swirled around me, but I couldn't tell if it came from Knox or Bishop or even myself. It just filled the air like fog rising from the ground, getting thicker and thicker until my skin buzzed with it.

Come here, Knox commanded in my head.

A snap of power crackled across my skin, but instead of making me go to him, it made my own strange power rise up in challenge as if this were a dream and not real life.

"Make me, alpha," I challenged.

His power snapped stronger, zinging along my nerves.

I gasped, the sensation sending heat rushing through my veins, and Knox's desire crushed through our bond.

Behind me, Bishop groaned, the sound a low, sexy rumbled that vibrated in his chest and against my back.

"Audrey," he purred. "He promised he'd be gentle with you because of your injuries. You might not want to tease him."

He skimmed his fingers up my sides, brushing the swell of my breasts and setting off my already sensitive nerves.

My breath caught on a moan and Bishop's need crashed over me, swirling with Knox's into a heady drug that had me instantly wet and aching.

"Teasing him teases you and me, and I'm not sure you're ready to handle both of our wolves when we're awake."

That thought sent more heat rushing to my core and my moan escaped.

"Not tonight," Bishop groaned, his voice strained. "I know you're sore and you're going to feel worse in the morning."

"Not if both of you fuck me," I breathed, feeling bold and confident. These were my mates and they wanted me. I could feel it whirling and teasing inside me, building my own need into an achy fire just waiting to explode into an inferno.

AUDREY

N*OT FUCK,* K*NOX* CORRECTED AS HE STALKED TOWARD US and shifted into his human form so he stood mere inches from me, gloriously naked, his cock full and proud. "We're not going to fuck you. We're going to make love. Tonight. I need to protect you, make sure you're safe."

"I *am* safe. I'm with my mates."

"I know you are," he growled back. "But still—"

He dipped forward and captured my lips in a soft kiss. I could feel his wildness and need rushing within him and stuttering through our mating bond, but I could also feel his need to protect me, even from himself.

"You're hurt and I won't hurt you more," he said, his voice low as he drew me toward the nest in the pergola. "But I need you."

"I need you, too," I murmured, letting him lead me with Bishop staying close behind me.

We reached the edge of the blanket and Knox pulled

me closer. His hard cock pressed against my belly, trapped between us, and he brushed his lips against mine. I could feel him fighting to stay in control and not let his wolf take over. And while I didn't care if his wolf took over — I trusted his wolf — I knew he needed to do this. He needed to show me he could be gentle and loving as much as he was wild and commanding.

I sank into his embrace and submitted to his gentleness. He'd been gentle when he'd gone down on me when Sterling had tricked me into hurting myself, so I already knew he was capable of it, but I sensed he needed to prove that to himself.

Behind me, Bishop pressed close and teased his lips over our mating bond, capturing me between them, two men who looked identical but loved me in their own unique ways.

The heat in my core grew hotter, and I moaned at Bishop's attention and kissed Knox back, letting my emotions, my love and desire and burning need for them, flood our bonds.

"Fuck," Knox growled breaking our kiss and jerking away from me.

His breathing was fast, his pupils fully dilated, almost dark enough to suggest his wolf was taking over, but I knew it wasn't. I could feel the beast coloring the emotions rushing between us, could feel its need to possess me and brand himself body, mind, and soul to me, but I could also feel its understanding of Knox's need to be gentle.

Bishop cupped my cheek and turned my head so I could kiss him over my shoulder, his lips taking over where Knox's had stopped. Bishop's desire was just as thick through our mating bond as his brother's, and his kiss hungrier. He plunged his tongue into my mouth, making me gasp, turning the heat within me into an inferno.

"Gorgeous," he praised as he pulled away and undid the ties at the back of my dress.

The garment slid down my body, pooling around my feet and ankles, and Knox's eyes followed the dress's movement, getting darker and darker the lower he looked.

"You have stitches," Knox said.

His voice was so low and filled with darkness, I could barely understand him, but the possessive protectiveness rolling through our mating bond like a thunderstorm about to let loose assured me he wasn't angry at me.

I grabbed his chin and urged him to meet my gaze.

"I earned them," I said, letting both Knox and Bishop feel my pride. "I defended our pack. I am *not* weak."

The words surged like liquid power through my veins and my alpha power unfurled around me.

I might have been shy, uncertain, and afraid, but I wasn't weak. Not anymore.

"You never were." Bishop brushed his lips against the back of my neck. "You're brave and capable. You care so deeply for those who can't protect themselves and I love that about you."

Love and pride surged through my bond with Bishop and joy bubbled inside me.

"You did such a good job protecting those children," Bishop said as his hand inched up my belly toward my breasts. "And you've handled yourself wonderfully with the delegates and their aides."

The joy flared stronger, jolting desire in my core, every word fueling the aching inside me.

Logically I knew I shouldn't need anyone's approval to feel good about myself, but the broken part of my soul craved it. And with Bishop's low sexy voice in my ear and his hands on me while Knox was kissing me as if I were the most precious thing in the world, I'd never felt more loved and accepted and seen.

Knox broke off our kiss with a growl, his desire heavy and thick in our bond, and his nostrils flared, taking in my scent.

Embarrassment flickered through me, an involuntary reaction born from my life before my mates.

"Don't," Knox barked with a snap of power that didn't control me, only made my own power flare stronger. "You smell so good."

He dropped to his knees, buried his nose in my curls, and inhaled deeply.

More wet heat pooled between my thighs, and I cracked my legs open, letting my desire perfume the air.

"Fuck," Knox hissed as he grabbed the back of my thighs and pushed his nose in deeper.

Bishop grabbed my hips and lifted me up, and Knox

pushed my legs over his shoulders, fully opening me
to him.

His tongue swept through my folds in a long lick that
finished with a barely-there flick against my clit, sending
more arousal rushing to my core. A responding lust burst
through our bonds as Knox lapped at my juices, our
alpha powers twirling and sliding against each other in a
slow, sensual dance.

Bishop groaned at the double blast of need from me
through our mating bond and Knox through their twin
bond. His erection, still captured in his pants, pressed
against the crack between my cheeks, sending another
thrill rushing through me.

What would that be like? Would I enjoy having him
push inside me through my puckered hole while Knox
was buried deep in my channel?

The thrills turned to molten heat. I wanted both of
them inside me, wanted the three of us to be so
completely joined for a glorious blissful moment that I
didn't know where either of us began or ended.

"Oh, gorgeous," Bishop purred. "What are you
thinking?"

The heat of embarrassment rushed across my cheeks,
but I quickly shoved it down and pressed back against
him as best I could.

"I was thinking—"

Knox teased his tongue inside me and my hips
bucked forward.

"You were thinking?" Bishop teased, moving a hand

from my waist — letting Knox take more of my weight — and plucking my nipple.

Pleasure shot from that tightened bud to my core, and I rolled my head back as I swallowed a moan.

"What were you thinking?" Bishop asked.

Knox flicked his tongue on my clit and slowly slid a finger inside me, and the moan I was holding back escaped.

"I was thinking of both of you."

"We should be all you're thinking about right now." Bishop plucked my nipple harder, this time adding just a bit of pain to my pleasure, twisting my need higher.

"I was thinking..." I panted as Knox pushed a second finger inside me all while sucking and licking my clit.

My hips bucked faster, my desire tightening, drawing closer to the edge, something both of them could feel through our bonds.

"Of both of you— inside me." Hints of stars flickered behind my lids and I fought to finish my sentence. "At the same time."

AUDREY

Surprise flashed through both of the bonds followed by heavy, consuming lust, along with a flare of alpha power. The sensation sent me crashing over the edge. Knox licked and sucked me through a release that was heightened by the need rolling through my mating bonds.

"You promise?" Knox asked, his gruff voice rumbling through my folds. "You really want that?"

"More than anything," I breathed.

With a growl, he dropped my thighs, grabbed my waist, and rolled back, sliding me onto his thick, hard cock in one smooth stroke.

His pleasure at being buried within me sent a mini orgasm rolling through me, and I gasped, knowing my first full orgasm had just been an appetizer.

Knox might not want to make love to me with his

usual ferocity because of injuries that weren't hurting at all at the moment, but that didn't matter. I was already hypersensitive, already halfway to an incredible release, and he could have done the bare minimum at the softest setting and I'd go off, screaming, in no time.

Satisfaction blazed through our bond, and he smirked at me despite him being in the more submission position beneath me.

His grip on my hips tightened, holding me in place, and slowly — so damned slowly as if he'd taken a lesson out of Bishop's playbook — he pulled out to just the tip then pushed back in.

My need tightened with just that stroke.

God, he felt so good.

Then Bishop sank to the blanket behind me and ran a heavy hand down my spine. Shivers followed where he touched me, turning into a fiery need when he cupped my ass.

A moan escaped my lips, and my head rolled back to rest on his chest, anticipation of him joining Knox inside me twisting my desire tighter.

"Wrong direction, beautiful," Bishop murmured in my ear as Knox pulled out and pushed back in, his girth raking against my sensitive channel. "This way."

Bishop leaned forward, forcing me to lie against Knox's chest, and placed my hands on either side of Knox's head.

Knox thrust again and again, his pace still slow and

deliberate as aching, desperate need poured through my bonds.

Bishop ran his hand down my spine again, drawing another heated shiver, and this time didn't stop to cup my ass. Instead, his fingers dipped to where Knox was torturing me, playing with my folds and clit.

My desire spun tighter and my breath picked up. I tried to rock down to meet Knox's thrusts but his grip was too strong.

Then Bishop slid a finger, slick with my desire, up to my hole. I jolted at the sensation even though I ached for his touch, and he teased the tight ring of muscle, quickly melting the jolt into pleasure.

Knox continued to thrust, his impatience and need seeping through our bond as he picked up his pace, while Bishop teased more of my juices to my hole.

I gasped and mewled, my need building, the fire that had barely cooled from my first orgasm blazing into an inferno. I needed harder, faster, more more more.

Please. Oh, please.

It wasn't enough, just a torturous tease holding me at aching but never growing into something more.

"You're doing great, gorgeous," Bishop purred, and the pad of his finger pushed against my hole.

Knox thrust again, the stroke more powerful than the last, and Bishop's finger slid inside me with a tingling, heated burn.

A full body shiver rolled through me, raising me from aching to desperate, and my channel started to flutter.

"Stop," Bishop barked.

A blast of his power froze me and Knox stopped mid-thrust, stealing my orgasm.

"Not yet." Bishop pushed his finger all the way in.

My eyes rolled back and I moaned while Knox growled, his body trembling with the effort to keep still.

The tension of not moving, of my aching need roiling with Knox's and Bishop's and our alpha powers whirling around us, twisted me tighter and tighter.

"Bishop, please," I begged. "I need you."

"Not like this," he said, as he slid his finger out and pushed back in. "You're not ready for anyone here. Not yet."

"But—"

He pulled out and pushed two fingers inside with a stronger heated burn that only added to my aching need.

"Soon. We'll work up to it. I'm not going to hurt you."

He leaned over me and brushed his lips over our mating mark while sliding his fingers out then in again.

Lust and determination teased through my bond with him and my channel started to flutter again in anticipation. I couldn't wait to have both of them, to be thoroughly joined with them.

Knox grunted and completed his thrust with a force that jolted through my bond and pushed Bishop's fingers deep inside me. Pleasure roared through my veins and flushed my skin, stealing my breath.

Oh, yes. More.

I wanted more of that. More force, more possession. I

liked when my guys claimed me, liked feeling their need for me and only me.

Knox's thrusts grew fast and hard, his control shattering, and Bishop worked my hole, pushing and scissoring, both of them building an ache inside me that twisted tighter and tighter. Every stroke quickly took me higher, up to a grand precipice that I knew meant I'd see stars when I finally came.

Then Knox's control shattered, and with a roar, he buried himself within me. Pleasure erupted through our bond, and with a scream, I flew off the precipice, soaring into a darkness filled with sparkling green flecks, a match to his and Bishop's eyes.

Bliss pounded through me, whirling me around and around, as I could feel Knox's hot jets of cum fill me, connecting with a primal need inside me.

I ground down on him, my core milking him, hungry for every last drop.

The second Knox was spent, Bishop shoved me against his brother's chest and jerked my hips back. Knox's cock slipped out and Bishop replaced him with a vicious stroke that was more Knox's style than his.

Then the dam Bishop had been keeping around his emotions, one I hadn't even realized had been there, shattered, and I could feel his ferocious need. He needed to fill me—

No, his wolf's need. His wolf had been patient, had agreed with Bishop what was best for us in the beginning, but now it was his turn.

He drove into me, giving me the harder and faster I'd ached for earlier. I moaned and gasped, trapped between the two of them, feeling deliciously possessed.

Alpha power crackled around us, stronger and sharper than when I'd been riding Knox. It tormented my sensitive flesh and made Knox's cock, which was trapped between us, harden.

"Fuck," he snarled, his hips bucking up to grind himself into my belly as Bishop drove into me.

Pleasure snapped along my spine and ricocheted to my core. Each powerful thrust raked through my channel, ending at the perfect spot deep inside me that made stars flash across my sight.

"You're so fucking beautiful," Bishop's wolf growled. "You take my cock beautifully, you gasp beautifully, and your scream when you come will be beautiful."

He drove harder, pounding me into Knox who shifted down a bit so when he bucked up, the base of his cock ground against my clit.

Sensation whirled through me, the press of their bodies capturing me, possessing me, protecting me. I didn't want to be without these men, didn't want to think or feel or even live. They were mine. They filled my soul with love and friendship and safety. They were home.

I was home.

Bishop's pace picked up, his thrusts growing uneven, but I didn't care. He and Knox had taken me to the highest precipice and stars already flashed through my vision.

Each powerful thrust and grind against my clit twisted nerves that were already achingly tight closer and closer to the breaking point.

Then Bishop yanked me up, capturing my back against his chest, thrust hard into me, and sank his teeth into my shoulder. I ground down on Knox, and together, all three of us cried out with our release.

The stars in my vision overwhelmed my sight, alpha power erupted around us electrifying my nerves, and I screamed. It was the only way to release all the glorious pressure.

My thoughts whirled, spinning me around and around in a whirlwind of bliss. Flecks of green stars and heady alpha power filled me, and deep satisfaction crashed through my mating bonds.

We collapsed together in a heap, Bishop aware enough to pull the edge of the blanket over top of us.

"I love you," Knox said, his voice a low satisfied grumbled that made my heart swell.

"I love you, too," I whispered, sending love through the bonds to both of them.

Tomorrow we'd still have to deal with the aftermath of the grimalkin attack and the merchants with their monster killing weapons, who my instincts said I should be wary of, but for right now, I was happy and thoroughly satisfied.

I was with my mates... well almost all my mates — something I wasn't going to think about right now — and needed to stay in this glorious moment. Anything could happen tomorrow, and I needed to hold onto feeling safe and happy and not worry about the future... even if I knew there were things to worry about.

CYRUS

I paced my office, waiting for Bishop to arrive. The sun had barely crept above the horizon, but I'd already been up for hours. Hell, I shouldn't have even bothered trying to go to bed. My mind hadn't settled and I'd barely gotten a few hours of terrible sleep.

Damn it. I felt like everything was spiraling out of control.

Like *I* was spiraling out of control.

I'd caught a glimmer of gold last night and turned to look out the ballroom door and Audrey had been standing there. I hadn't thought she could look more beautiful than when she'd shown up for the city tour yesterday morning wearing a dress that matched the flecks in Bishop's eyes and was designed to show off her mating marks. But last night she'd been breathtaking.

And now I couldn't stop thinking about her, couldn't stop remembering how it felt to bury myself inside her tight, hot sheath, and how my wolf had almost claimed her.

And of course, I hadn't had time to talk with her about anything. I'd had to rush away to deal with the fallout of the attack. And I'd left with a "we need to talk."

Which was the stupidest thing I could have said.

Even I knew you didn't say that to a woman after sex. You told her how beautiful she was, how much you cared about her. Hell, I could have even talked about wanting to protect her — although I had a feeling that would have come out wrong, too.

But no. My alpha mask had slammed into place the second I'd realized I'd lost control of myself and needed to be focusing on the most urgent matter: the aftermath of the grimalkin attacks and those merchants with their dangerous weapons that I felt we had no choice but to buy.

Except that only made me think of everything else going on: helping the injured and those who'd lost loved ones, proper burials, and the deaths of the fighters from the alliance, which I prayed wouldn't turn into a political incident.

Thankfully, Folmar wouldn't demand reparations for Cohnal's injuries even though I could tell she was heart-broken. He was a good man, but their pride wouldn't accept him now as alpha mate — since their primary alphas were always women. No gryphon alpha female would think he, blind in one eye and missing half a leg, would be a worthy mate.

I sighed. Audrey would be so upset when she learned of all that. He'd heroically taken on three grimalkins by himself to protect her along with the women and children in that small square. He'd managed to kill all of them before help had arrived, and Audrey would be pissed that he was going to be punished for it, even if it wasn't an intentional punishment. I'd seen her speak with him during the tour, so I knew she knew him, even if it was just casual. Hell, even if she hadn't known him, she'd still be upset because that was the generous soul that was my mate—

Not my mate.

Not yet.

Someone knocked on my office door and opened it without waiting for my response.

"Good," I said as Bishop walked in.

"What's the plan for today?" he asked, closing the door and pacing to the windows behind my desk.

"Is Knox with her?" I blurted out before I realized what I was saying.

Sisters! I was supposed to be talking about the alliance meetings today because the attacks had changed the agenda.

"They're in bed in her suite," he replied, the corner of his lips twitching.

"There's still an assassin on the loose," I said, and his smile vanished, which wasn't what I'd meant to say, either. Damn it.

I raked my hands over my head, already feeling the braid I wore to keep it out of my eyes loosening.

"That wasn't— I didn't mean—" I blew out a heavy breath.

I wasn't going to be able to keep her off my mind and focus on everything else.

She was my mate. And while she'd proven she was strong and capable when things were desperate, I couldn't stop the instincts screaming inside me saying I needed to protect her... and claim her.

Except there was no way she'd accept me as a mate, not with how I'd treated her. And she shouldn't. She deserved better. It didn't matter if we could both feel something between us. It didn't matter that she'd submitted to my wolf and enjoyed herself in the shower. That didn't mean she accepted me as a mate.

Which meant I needed to court her... one of the things I was an absolute disaster at.

"We need to talk business," I said, my voice gruff. "But you have to tell me how to court Audrey first. I'm losing my mind. There's so much going on, and all my wolf cares about is protecting and claiming."

"And what do *you* want?" Bishop asked.

I stared at the gardens outside my office window, unable to look him in the eyes. He was Audrey's mate, fated to be with her just like Knox was. I'd slept with her a few times now, and her soul hadn't claimed me like it had claimed them. Still—

"She's my mate. *Our* mate," I said.

"No more pushing her away," he replied.

"That's why I need your advice. I open my mouth and I always say the wrong thing."

"You know that's not true."

I stared at him. "My wolf took over and we had sex in the hospital staff shower room. What did I say after when Deacon called me away?"

"You didn't," Bishop groaned already knowing it was going to be something stupid. This wasn't my first time saying the wrong thing to a woman and I doubted it would be my last.

"We need to talk." I raked my fingers through my hair, pulling out most of the braid. "We need to talk. Who says that after sex? Who says that after my wolf almost sank our teeth into her and claimed her?"

"Sisters, Cyrus," Bishop said. "At least you didn't bite her."

"No shit." We wouldn't have bonded, and I'd have just given her another scar, not the mating mark my wolf wanted. She had to accept us first, and that would never happen if I kept doing what I was doing.

"The first thing you need to do is apologize." Bishop leveled a hard look at me. "And do it from the heart. You can't be in control of this."

"I know." My insides squirmed at the thought.

I was the one in charge, the responsible one. *I* took on those burdens so no one else had to, but I knew the tiny voice inside me, begging me to surrender, was right. I just had no idea how to let go.

"Should I get her flowers? Sweets? How do I show her I mean it, that I'm sorry and I'd be a good mate?"

Bishop was so good with women. He always knew the right thing to say and do. Hell, he did it unconsciously and half the females in the pack were in love with him... which was another potential danger for Audrey.

Fuck.

I bit back a growl. Why did I always go there? Why was I constantly thinking of dangers? That couldn't be what I focused on with Audrey. My wolf might think protecting our mate was the only thing that mattered, but even I knew that wasn't the way to win her heart.

She needed mates who believed in her and thought she was strong and competent, even if her strengths weren't physical... because they *weren't* physical. Her strengths were kindness and empathy.

"You need to be honest with her and vulnerable."

My wolf jerked our head toward Bishop and snarled. We did *not* reveal vulnerabilities. We were alpha. The pack needed to know their leader was strong.

"You need to tell her how you feel and why you've been a dick to her," Bishop continued, ignoring my wolf's warning. "And you need to do it without pride and without being defensive. You need to treat her like you're treating me right now."

"I'm not treating her like she's my brother."

"No, you should treat her like an equal and a confidant." Bishop's expression softened. "That's what a mate is. A partner, an equal, someone you trust implicitly, and someone who doesn't judge you for your flaws."

Which was exactly what Bishop and Audrey were to each other. It didn't mean he didn't have to apologize or work to keep their relationship alive and healthy. It meant that they talked it out when something went wrong, and that they had each other's backs when dealing with everyone else.

Me being overprotective undermined Audrey and her relationships. She already had a protector she trusted in Knox and a lover who worshiped her in Bishop. My role was to be her equal, to prove to her I trusted her and valued her opinions, to show her she was and always would be worthy.

And all I needed to do was let go and trust.

AUDREY

I WOKE TO FEATHER-SOFT KISSES ALONG MY JAW AND disappointment whispering through my mate bond with Knox.

"I have to go," he said as I cracked open one eye and fell into the bottomless depths of his gaze.

"The room—" I started, about to say I understood he had to go outside. Except I couldn't feel the churning unease that Knox always felt when he'd reached his limit for staying indoors.

"Patrol duty," he huffed. "I think I could stay here with you for another couple of hours."

Which was amazing. Sure, the dinner had gone until after sunset and we'd cuddled under the stars after making love before returning to my suite, so we hadn't been here all night. But Knox's time inside should have been up by now.

"It's you," he said, his voice gruff as he nuzzled the sensitive spot behind my ear. "You settle my soul."

Peace and relief washed through the bond. He'd been struggling with his claustrophobia for years and while I hadn't cured it — and doubted I ever would — I'd helped to ease some of the pressure. He had more choice now about how he could live his life, and that made me happy.

"You have to get up, too."

"Right, eavesdropping on alliance stuff," I groaned, wishing I could have another hour— hell, even thirty minutes to stay in bed with my mate, while praying I'd have some free time to talk to Whil.

Because I *had* to talk to Whil about the grimalkins and smoke soon. I didn't want to neglect my problems and have them make everything worse.

Knox looked at me expectantly, waiting for... something.

"You don't have to show me the way. I need to shower first, so I'll just go to the kitchen," I said, dragging myself into an upright position and feeling not nearly as sore as I expected after sex with Bishop and Knox and surviving a fight with three grimalkins. "Eloise or Kira can tell me where to go."

"No," he huffed. "You don't go anywhere alone."

"The grimalkins didn't get anywhere close to the Residence," I protested. "I'll be fine."

But worry poured through our bond and didn't ease up at my words.

"Someone tried to kill you and they're still out there."
A growl rumbled in his chest and he hugged me tight.
"We're short watchmen and hunters. I have to patrol. But you're not safe without me or Bishop."

A shiver rolled down my spine at the memory of that person attacking and poisoning Bishop. With everything going on, Bishop and Cyrus couldn't spare the time to search for the assailant.

Whoever it was had caught me and Bishop alone, at night, on a dimly lit street. Surely, he wouldn't attack in broad daylight while I was in the Residence.

Except I knew anything was possible and anyone who I didn't know could be the assassin. I could only hope they were going to be more cautious now that Bishop had lived and could identify him by his scent.

And Bishop knowing the assailant's scent didn't rule out everyone in the pack. The Stonehaven pack was large and it would be impossible for the alphas to have memorized everyone's scent.

"Okay," I agreed. "Give me five minutes to shower."

Knox huffed his agreement, and I hurried out of bed, powered through a shower, and changed into a cream-colored dress — one of many that had appeared in my wardrobe between dinner last night and this morning.

This dress was simpler than the previous two I'd worn, without any embroidery, but it still had the higher-than-regular back and thinner-than-regular neck strap to show off my mating marks.

I braided my hair to keep it out of the way and to hopefully look more serious and confident — as if I actually belonged in the alliance's meeting. Then Knox shifted into his wolf and we left my suite through the French doors and walked around the back of the castle to the herb garden and the kitchen door.

All the delegates are taking breakfast in the ballroom, Knox said in my head. *But Bishop said you'd rather eat in the kitchen.*

I gave Knox a grateful smile, knowing he could feel my relief through the bond. I knew I had to spend the next however-many days in the spotlight, having everyone watching me even if I didn't say a word, and I hadn't been looking forward to it.

Just thinking about all those people staring at me, wondering why I was Bishop's and Knox's mate or why I was even in the room made my insides twist.

I'd spent my life trying to be as small and unnoticed as possible and now I had to take up space. An alpha's mate didn't shrink from scrutiny. She faced it head on. Or at least that's what I felt an alpha's mate did. I could be soft and not draw attention to myself, but I couldn't be small anymore.

I didn't *want* to be small.

But I also knew it was going to take time and practice — not to mention be emotionally draining — to go against everything I'd been taught.

I needed to be kind and patient with myself just like I was with the children.

Love and worry crept through my bond with Knox while Bishop's connection held a hint of concern.

I sent my love back to them.

I could do this.

And I wasn't alone.

Knox left me in the kitchen's doorway, bounding out of the garden and heading toward the front of the castle, and I turned to head inside through the open kitchen door.

But Velora stepped through the hall entrance into the kitchen, and I jerked back, pressing my back against the rough, stone wall beside the doorway.

Worry and shame fought for control inside me. I shouldn't have been afraid of Velora. I *wanted* to stand my ground. But I also didn't want to cause a scene and embarrass Cyrus and Bishop in front of the alliance delegates.

And not because it wasn't my place or I was afraid they'd get mad, but because a responsible person didn't air their private business in front of political guests.

I wasn't sure what relationship my guys had with the other leaders, but I refused to be the reason other countries and kingdoms and any other foreign whatever looked down on our pack.

A lot was going on right now, and adding a cat fight between the alpha mate and one of the pack's betas wouldn't help anything.

And that was what it would end up being.

Even if Velora reminded me of where she thought my

place was and criticized me, it wasn't to protect the pack. She wanted Bishop, and I'd taken him, and after the look she'd given me when Bishop had pointed out our mating mark, I wasn't sure anyone could make her see reason.

Which was just another problem on top of all the others Bishop and Cyrus had to deal with.

I let my gaze slide over the herb garden as I listened to Velora order breakfast from Kira. She wasn't mean to the cook's assistant but there was still a clear edge of superiority in her tone.

It made the wildness inside me bubble up. How dare she treat Kira as though she was less than her?

Except if I stormed in to protect Kira—

Movement on the far side of the herb garden caught my attention and everything within me froze.

One of the merchants, the short, stocky one strolled past the garden farther from the Residence. That, in and of itself, wasn't an issue. Bishop had mentioned that there was going to be a leaders' only meeting in the morning. No aides or merchants, only translators. It was the tightness and wariness in the merchant's body language that bothered me.

He was trying to look natural, but the *trying* was giving him away with movement that looked rehearsed and repetitive. A glance at a flowering bush, a pause at a tree then another glance and another pause.

Maybe he was just uncomfortable being at the Residence with all the political leaders. I certainly was. Or maybe he was worried about selling the weapons.

But my wildness rejected those explanations. He was up to something and I wanted to know what.

I glanced back in the kitchen to see Velora's back to me while she supervised Kira's cooking, so I crept out of sight of the open kitchen door and after the merchant.

The stocky man in his silky embroidered robe slunk along the hedgerow of another garden then another, going deeper and deeper into the Residence's grounds until he was almost at the towering rock wall at the back.

Three other merchants, dressed in similar clothing waited for him... which was weird. Bishop had said there were only three merchants. That, and I recognized the guy I'd followed and the other two from the town tour, but not the big, muscular man with the dark glare.

"I thought I said ten minutes after their meeting started," the muscular merchant I didn't recognize said.

"The idiot, Jundar, cornered me in the hall," the guy I'd followed replied. "He's interested in making a deal even if the rest of the ridiculous alliance isn't."

"Good," one of the two tall and lanky merchants said. He wore a deep crimson robe with black embroidery, which made his pale skin and short white-blond hair stand out in stark contrast.

"What about the others?" the muscular merchant asked, his voice dropping, making him harder to hear.

I crept closer and knelt beside a large bush, straining to hear their conversation.

"On the fence," the other lean guy said. He wore an olive-green robe with gold embroidery that partially camouflaged him against the rock and trees. "Even Gower. We knew the gryphons, wolves, and Dedearc were going to be a tough sell, but Gower surprised me."

"He's too dependent on the wolves even though the mutts aren't as strong as the gryphons and our grimalkins put the gryphon's heir in the hospital," Muscles said, a vicious, satisfied gleam in his eyes.

My heart stuttered.

Holy shit!

I clamped my hands over my mouth to muffle my gasp. Surely, I'd heard that wrong. *Their* grimalkins? *They* were responsible for the attack?

Were they also responsible for the previous attack? The one that had killed those children?

"I think they need another push," the stocky one said gleefully. "If we prove that these wolves can't even protect their town, Gower will realize he has to buy our weapons."

"They'll get suspicious if another pack attacks so soon," Green Robe said.

"No," Muscles barked. "Emrys is right. They're going to want to talk about all of this for days. Cyrus and Folmar are too cautious and Jundar too eager. They'll butt heads, get all worked up, and *then* we'll release another pack to seal the deal."

"I've already moved our other pack to the pens in Anakar," Red Robe said. "But after that, we'll have to wait four more months for the next litter to be ready."

"That's fine," Muscles replied. "One more push and

they'll be falling all over themselves to buy our weapons. Start sowing discord. Let Jundar think Gower and Cyrus don't trust him and whisper around Cyrus's betas that Jundar and Pimryl are thinking of buying in secret, that they want to take over the alliance."

The other three nodded and hurried back toward the Residence while Muscles stood there, his lips twisted in a wicked grin.

I hugged myself tighter, squeezing into the smallest, stillest ball possible, my heart pounding so hard I was sure he, even with his human hearing, could hear it.

Stay calm, I told myself. *Keep your emotions to yourself.* Because the last thing I needed was for Bishop or Knox to come storming back here.

If I could stay hidden, I could tell Bishop and Cyrus what I'd overheard and we'd have the advantage. But that only worked if Muscles didn't know that I'd overheard him.

I just needed to wait until Muscles left.

He chuckled and the wind shifted, carrying the dark reek of the grimalkins along with a whisp of black smoke. I glanced through the bushes as he turned to follow the path around the outside edge of the Residence's grounds, catching a red glimmer in his eyes and another curl of smoke.

Shivers rushed down my spine, my wildness wanting to rise up and defend me, but knowing staying hidden was my best option.

Something was wrong with that man. He was dangerous, more dangerous than just the lightning weapons he and his fellow merchants were selling.

BISHOP

My brother was an idiot. I saw the realization in his expression back in his office, knew he knew what he had to do to win Audrey over, and yet we were still in the scheduled alliance meeting.

He should have postponed everything, even for just fifteen minutes, and checked in on Audrey. He didn't have to grovel and woo her right away, but he needed little acts of consideration, small ways of showing her he was thinking of her to get him going.

Except she hadn't shown up in the dining room for breakfast, most likely wanting to stay away from the public scrutiny for as long as possible, and Cyrus hadn't sought her out.

Of course, she also wasn't in the meeting, and I'd specifically told Eloise and Kira to tell Audrey to join us.

Even more concerning were her muted emotions, making it impossible to tell exactly what she was feeling other than a sense of soft worry — something I often felt from Audrey that didn't necessarily mean there was anything wrong except she usually wasn't trying to block those feelings from me.

I ground my teeth, resisting the urge to glare at Cyrus for being an idiot, and fought to focus on the alliance members.

It was just the six of us, along with a translator for Jundar and Pimryl. We sat at a round table so no one looked like they were in charge even though Jundar was supposed to be the one who ensured things remained civil and ran smoothly. And while the setting was more casual, everyone was still dressed as if this were a formal meeting.

"The weapons are amazing," Jundar said through his translator, the medals on his crisp military jacket catching the sunlight that poured through the open window.

"Those weapons destroyed buildings in one shot," Folmar growled back, her expression a mix of determination and exhaustion. "They're dangerous."

"With the proper training—" Jundar started but Gower cut him off.

"I don't think we should be debating whether we buy the weapons or not." The muscles in Gower's jaw flexed. "If we don't, we're opening ourselves up for retaliation."

"You honestly think Emrys and his fellow merchants would attack us?" Jundar asked.

I took in a breath to tell him of course Emrys would

attack — hadn't the man been paying attention? — when a burst of worry shot through my mating bond before returning to its previous muted level.

What the—?

"Given how he didn't seem upset every time he missed with his weapon, it wouldn't surprise me," Cyrus said, his tone low and cold. "I know that he's personally responsible for the deaths of three of my pack."

Jundar opened his mouth but wisely snapped it shut.

Yeah, arguing with Cyrus about how accidents happen in the kind of fight we'd just faced and how the merchants probably prevented more people from dying wasn't going to help.

"I understand both your concerns," Pimryl said, her soft tone always a surprising contradiction with her size — which was bigger than Cyrus who was one of the biggest men in our pack — along with her fierce lizard-like features.

"Speaker Jundar," she continued. "I can understand how attractive these weapons are for you. Humans are at the greatest disadvantage against grimalkins. But you're right, Alpha Cyrus, these weapons are dangerous. We need to determine if proper training will improve accuracy or find an alternative to help our physically weaker alliance members. They want to be able to protect themselves and not have to rely so strongly on our warriors."

Jundar stiffened at Pimryl's insult — even if it was true — and Gower rolled his eyes.

I shifted in my seat, Audrey's worry still muted but

growing stronger as if she were losing her fight to contain her emotions.

"We should ask Emrys for a more structured demonstration," Folmar said. "See if we can determine if accuracy is actually a problem or if—"

Another burst of worry flooded the mating bond—no, *fear*. The emotion stuttering through the bond as if Audrey were trying to hide it from me was fear.

My heart lurched and I jumped to my feet before I realized what I was doing.

Bishop— Cyrus hissed before his eyes widened, realization hitting him — because the only thing that would make me run out of an alliance meeting was Audrey.

"Recess," he barked.

The startled alliance members glanced between us, confusion and surprise on their faces.

"We'll reconvene in an hour," Cyrus said as I raced for the door. "Pack emergency."

Folmar raised an eyebrow at us, a knowing glint in her eyes, but I didn't care if she knew we were rushing off to protect our mate or not. The others would judge us knowing we'd abruptly stopped the discussion for a woman and not a larger problem, but the gryphon alpha knew that we couldn't deny our primal instincts, not with me so newly mated and Cyrus trying to become her mate.

The fear in the bond tugged at me, and I raced down the hall and out the closest door onto the Residence's grounds. My pulse pounded with each step, her emotions getting stronger and stronger.

I had to get to Audrey now now now.

I couldn't let anything happen to her.

The pull around my heart led me deeper onto the Residence's grounds, past my mother's seasonal gardens toward the sheer rock wall at the back.

"What's she doing all the way back here?" Cyrus growled, his gaze scanning the area as the trees and bushes thickened into a more overgrown area.

"I don't—"

Determination and a hint of anger flooded around the fear, and a second later Audrey bolted out from behind a shrub and slammed into me.

I grabbed her before she could stumble back, holding her close to my chest, and she melted into my embrace.

"What's wrong?" Cyrus demanded, his eyes dark with his wolf, his body practically vibrating with his fight to stay in control.

"The merchants have grimalkins."

AUDREY

I TOLD BISHOP AND CYRUS — WHILE IGNORING THE ACHE IN my chest whenever I looked at Cyrus — what I'd overheard, and they hurried me back to the safety of the Residence. Somehow, I convinced Bishop, with Cyrus's agreement, that we couldn't bring what I'd overheard to the other members of the alliance. We needed more than just my say so. We needed proof.

Cyrus quickly dispatched Finn to call Deacon and Knox back to the Residence — since Deacon and Knox were out of even Cyrus's mental reach — and we returned to the leader's only alliance meeting, knowing we needed to buy us enough time to find that proof.

The rest of the day involved hours of discussion where I strained to sit still and look calm while trying to overhear snippets of whispered conversations, particularly among the merchants. But no one said anything that gave away more of the merchants' plans, and I ended the day exhausted and frustrated.

I'd been completely useless, and on top of that, I hadn't found a moment to look for Whil and ask about the smoke that had fluttered out of my mouth when I'd controlled the grimalkins. We hadn't even taken a break when Deacon and Knox returned to the Residence. Cyrus had used his telepathy to tell them what was going on and to search Anakar for proof, and we hadn't had to leave the meeting room.

Thankfully, the dinner ended early. I hadn't felt sick to my stomach or seen any smoke all day so I let Bishop lead me back to my suite where we undressed, cuddled on my bed, and fell asleep.

A few minutes later... or had it been an hour? Two hours? More? My eyes fluttered open.

I took in the familiar towering tree surrounding me, the moist earth and the sweet scent of pine needles. I was in my old pack's sacred grove.

A chill raced down my spine, settling hard and heavy in my gut. The last time I'd dreamed of this sacred grove, Sterling had tormented me, driving a knife into my greatest fears over and over again in an attempt to make me kill myself... because I was forever linked to that monster.

Whil had said she'd magically blocked the connection between us, but she hadn't been able to break it, and that could mean he was invading my dreams again.

My pulse lurched, and I glanced around, searching

for a way out of the grove even though I knew it was futile. If Sterling wanted me here, it wouldn't matter if I ran. I'd always end up where I started. I'd always be trapped.

No.

I clenched my jaw, determined to stay calm. It was just a dream. Sterling might be able to control it, but he couldn't affect my body in the waking world. I was still safe from him. We weren't even in the same realm.

The bushes on the far side of the grove rustled, and I scrambled into the underbrush at the edge of the grove, instinct making me hide in the shadows.

A second later, Sterling and Royce appeared, each carrying a slumped figure over their shoulder, one male and one female.

The male wheezed, weakly struggling in Royce's grip as if he were dazed, unable to do anything because his hands and ankles were tied, while the female didn't move at all.

With a grunt, Sterling dumped the woman into the center of the grove. Her long dark hair swept away from her face and my breath stalled in my lungs.

Mila. The only person brave enough to become my friend in my old pack. Sterling and Royce had laughed about tricking her into thinking she and her mate, Porter, had heard the fated mating call because they'd wanted to isolate me. And it had worked. I'd been alone for almost a year.

The guys had said Porter hadn't been involved in their

plans, just another unwitting dupe, and Mila had been happy at her mating ceremony, so why was I dreaming of them now?

Or rather, why was Sterling making me dream of them?

Mila groaned and rolled onto her back, her eyes glassy and unfocused as if she were drugged and Royce dumped the man beside her.

"Porter," she moaned, her gaze sliding to the man, her mate, who growled and rolled up to his knees.

"I don't think so," Royce snarled, grabbing Porter's head and slamming his knee into his face.

Mila gasped and Porter dropped to the ground, moaning.

"That's right," Royce said, kicking him in the ribs hard enough to send him sliding across the dirt. "Stay down."

Royce moved to kick him again, but Sterling growled, and a snap of alpha power exploded from him, making Royce freeze.

"I need their beating hearts," he said, his voice filled with menace.

Fear rushed through my body, freezing my breath in my lungs, and Royce dipped his head in submission.

Shadows and wisps of black smoke swirled around Sterling and red flickered in his eyes. Another crushing wave of alpha power roared through the grove, and Mila and Porter moaned while Royce sank to his knees.

I inched farther back into the underbrush despite the wildness inside me rising up and defying Sterling's demand to submit. So far, he hadn't noticed me and I wasn't going to draw attention to myself.

"Good," he laughed, the sound sending more shivers racing down my spine. "Now step back."

Royce scurried to the side of the grove, out of the circle of moonlight, and Sterling pulled a vial containing a red glowing liquid from his pocket.

Just like when he'd tried to sacrifice me to that monster, he dumped the liquid onto the ground and hissed, "Open, Gate of the Realms."

Magic exploded into the grove, crashing against me and stealing my breath. Mila and Porter moaned and Sterling threw his head back and howled with laughter. The power twisted into a whirlwind, picking up dead leaves and small stones while pulling oozing strands of black smoke from the ground. It spun higher and higher, pouring into the night sky and blotting out the stars and moon.

Thunder cracked, sharp and loud, making me jump, and Royce's gaze snapped toward me. I froze, praying he couldn't see me in the gloom. My pulse roared, everything within me screaming to run, get away, stop reliving the moment when I was offered up to a monster. I didn't want to watch Mila and her mate be eaten alive. It had been bad enough hearing it while the monster had been eating Merrick.

Except I knew the second I tried to escape, the dream would change and it wouldn't be Mila and Porter being sacrificed, it would be me.

Lightning sliced through the darkness and Sterling howled with manic joy, drawing Royce's attention. Porter heaved himself back to his knees and strained to break the rope binding his hands behind his back. Mila moaned and writhed, her breathing desperate, sharp gasps, her eyes clearer now as if the drugs were wearing off just in time for her to die.

Save them, Audrey, I screamed at myself. *Save them.*

No. Run!

Another crack of thunder shook me and more lightning sliced through the whirling smoke, tearing open an enormous column of shimmering air, a rip between my old realm and my new one.

Power poured through the rip, bringing with it the putrid reek of the grimalkins, and the smoke thickened. It embraced Sterling, while also rushing around me. It caressed me, resonated with something deep in my soul, and taunted me with how it had leaked from my mouth when I'd make the grimalkins run away.

I could feel the connection between us, the oozing smoke linking us together, the darkness growing inside both of us. Then Mila screamed, dragging my attention to the smoke tearing into her and Porter.

Sterling's laughter deepened and enormous, leathery wings ripped out the back of his shirt. A flush rushed over him, turning all visible skin red, just like the monster he'd summoned, and thick, black ram's horns grew from his temples.

"Yes," he roared, fire blazing from his eyes as he

stretched his arms wider and wider, his body growing bigger.

Thick long claws extended from his fingertips, longer and more vicious than a regular shifter's claws, and with a manic grin, he slammed his claws into Porter's chest, tearing into his flesh and ripping out his heart.

Oh, God.

Bile burned the back of my throat and my soul screamed at me.

Do something. Anything. Wake the fuck up.

I squeezed my eyes shut, straining to shut out Mila's panicked screams, Sterling's howls of laughter, and the roaring wind.

It's just a dream. Just a dream.

This wasn't really happening. Sterling wasn't becoming the monster he'd tried to sacrifice me to, and Mila and her mate were safe with his pack. She'd escaped our old pack. She was free.

This was just Sterling torturing me. I needed to wake up and get to Whil. Have her fix the block.

But a part of me, a small, terrified voice inside me, screamed that I was wrong. This was more than a dream.

AUDREY

My eyes flew open, and I jerked upright, my sheets stuck to my sweat-drenched body as I gasped for air.

"Audrey?" Bishop gasped, jerking upright a second later. "What's wrong?"

"I—" My throat tightened and I struggled to breathe.

It had just been a dream.

Except none of my dreams about Sterling had been *just* anything.

"I have to go to Whil. Now."

I glanced at the window but couldn't tell through the crack in the blinds if it was still the middle of the night or closer to dawn. I didn't want to bother Whil, but I couldn't risk the block in my mind being broken. If Sterling could influence me, I needed to know so I could protect my mates and my pack.

And I needed to know right now.

Bishop grabbed my dress from where it lay on the

floor and tossed it to me before pulling on his pants —
also on the floor where we'd left them.

"Talk to me, Audrey," he said, worry pouring through
our mating bond as we rushed out the French doors in
my sitting room.

"I think the block in my mind is breaking."

Please let it just be the block.

But I had a horrible feeling something else was
happening. I couldn't shake the ominous feeling inside
me or the hint of grimalkin reek caught in my nostrils.

Sterling hadn't tormented me like he had in the other
dreams. In fact, the more I thought about it, the more it
felt like he hadn't even been aware I'd been there.
Without a doubt, he'd have rubbed in how helpless I was
while he murdered Mila and Porter and opened a rip in
the realms to get to me.

My pulse lurched.

I'd dreamed he reopened the rip. Had the dream been
a threat... or reality?

Bishop and I rushed across the Residence's grounds
to Whil's cottage, the whimsical glass light hanging above
the doorway to the English cottage part of her residence
bright in the pre-dawn gray.

With a growl, Bishop banged his fist against the
cottage door, making me cringe.

"Whil!" he yelled as he threw open the door and
strode inside.

Two wall lamps in the entranceway flared to life,
revealing polished wood floors and clean white walls.

Straight ahead rose a staircase with a wooden banister carved to look like vines, and a long narrow hall led to the back of the house. To my left stood a wide arch opening into a sitting room.

I peered into the darkness at the end of the hall but couldn't see beyond the warm halo of light. Somewhere, farther back, lay the entrance to the massive greenhouse attached to the cottage.

"Whil," Bishop called again.

"Coming," she yelled back from somewhere above us.

Wood creaked at the top of the stairs, a pale light started to illuminate the walls, and a second later Whil appeared, her perpetual fae glow lighting her way.

"Audrey thinks the block is breaking," he said as Whil hurried down the stairs.

"Sit," she said, jerking her chin toward the archway beside us, "and tell me what happened."

"I had a dream," I told her, crossing the threshold into the sitting room and activating the three magical lamps in the room with my movement.

Three large armchairs and a couch as mismatched as the seating area in the greenhouse, crowded around a squat table covered with books, while more books and knickknacks filled the floor-to-ceiling bookcases taking up all available wall space. The only places where there wasn't a bookcase was the fieldstone fireplace on the interior wall and the two large windows overlooking Whil's perpetually blooming garden.

"And..." I sat on the couch knowing as soon as she

checked my magical block, I was going to pass out for most of the day. "And I think there's something else going on."

Bishop sat beside me and pulled me into his lap, holding me tight. Worry tinged with fear whispered through our bond despite the fact that I could feel him trying to block his emotions from me.

"I think I controlled the grimalkins and made them run away. They have an alpha power, and I could feel it, and when those last two came and I was barely hanging on, I screamed at them and, with my own power, willed them to go away," I said, the words pouring out of me.

"What did their power feel like?" Whil asked, and I released the breath I'd been holding even while knowing I hadn't needed to hold it.

Whil and Bishop had always believed me. I'd never had to convince them that what I'd experienced or felt was true.

"It made my skin crawl and upset my stomach and when I used my power on them, black smoke came out of my mouth."

Bishop stiffened, his grip around me tightening, and he buried his nose in my hair.

"It's been over a day," he said, his voice soft even as a torrent of emotions: fear, anger, and frustration roared through the bond. "You should have said something."

"Whil's been at the hospital, Knox is hunting, and you and Cyrus have been dealing with a crisis."

It wasn't as if I'd wanted to keep it a secret. I'd just

recognized that there were more important things going on, and I'd wanted to do my part and hadn't wanted to worry anyone.

"The nausea and smoke went away and I thought I could wait until I found a moment to talk to Whil." I leaned back far enough to meet his wolf-darkened eyes. "The second something changed, I told you."

"You should have told me right away," he growled. "You're the priority. You're always the priority."

"You know that isn't true," I said. "The pack—"

"The pack doesn't matter without you." He pressed his forehead to mine and drew in a shuddering breath. "I know you want to protect those who can't protect themselves and you think that sacrificing your needs is how to do that, but it isn't." He huffed. "I already have a brother who always puts himself last. I don't need my mate to do it, too."

More frustration rolled through our bond, and I pushed love back to him. We weren't going to agree on this, and I didn't want to argue. He could teach me how to put me first later, once the crisis with the merchants and grimalkins and whatever Sterling was doing to me was taken care of.

"Whil," I said without turning away from Bishop. "Let's find out what's going on with me."

AUDREY

Whil placed her hands on my temples, and, just like all the other times she'd checked her magic blocking the tether connecting me to Sterling, I took a breath and released it. Her warm, golden power seeped into my head, muddling my thoughts, and I sank back against Bishop.

I drifted on a golden haze, savoring the peace that came with it. For a blissful moment all my worries about what was happening to me and the pack were gone and I felt safe and loved.

Then the haze melted away and I opened my eyes.

I lay on the short, old-fashioned couch in the greenhouse, and Whil sat on the floor a few feet away surrounded by books. Bishop must have carried me out here so Whil could do research while keeping an eye on me.

The sun sat high in the sky, but that didn't surprise

me. Whenever Whil checked the block, I lost half a day. Bishop was also gone, which I'd expected. He had pack responsibilities and couldn't sit around all morning waiting for me to wake up.

"So," I groaned as I dragged myself up into a seated position.

Whil glanced up from her book, her expression grim.

That wasn't good.

I focused on my mating bonds. Knox's bond was there but emotionless since he wasn't close enough for me to sense, and Bishop's was muted with only a hint of determination and worry. Which didn't tell me at all if Whil had told Bishop what she'd discovered or not.

"My magic is still blocking the tether," Whil said. "But it's definitely weaker."

"And?" I asked, since still being cut off from Sterling wasn't grounds to be grim.

"The tether has evolved. It's now not just a link between you two, it's also a magical power source," Whil replied. "A dark magic power source."

"Dark magic?" A shiver raced through me despite the humid warmth in the greenhouse.

"Yes, whatever the son of your old pack's alpha did, it's growing in strength."

My stomach churned. I wasn't just tethered to Sterling for the rest of my life, I was caught up in the spell he'd cast to gain more power from that monster.

Oh, God. The last time I'd seen Sterling, he'd had ghostly ram's horns just like the monster. His face had also turned red, but I'd thought that was because he was angry. Now I wasn't so sure.

In my dream, he'd actually become the monster, and that dream had felt too real as if I were witnessing Mila and Porter's murder, not just imagining it. That menacing power had filled the air and caressed my skin, calling out to something inside me, something that rang in recognition.

Was I going to become that monster, too?

The grimalkin's alpha power had felt similar to the power Sterling had used to send those snake shadow monsters after us, a power that had already been hanging in the air around us in Anakar and the surrounding forest.

"Can you get rid of it? Block it?" I asked even as a new horrible thought occurred to me.

I'd run into this realm a weak, pathetic shifter. And now I had power.

Was the power actually mine? Was I actually a female alpha trapped behind a curse that was starting to crumble?

Or was it because of the dark power growing inside me?

If Whil got rid of it, would I go back to being me?

"I tried strengthening the block I already put on the tether," Whil said, "but it isn't strong enough to stop the power from seeping into you." She swept her hands out at the books surrounding her. "I'm researching alternatives."

"We have to tell the guys." As much as I didn't want to add more to their plate, me turning into a monster was important. "I should probably be confined."

"Bishop said you'd say that and has made it clear that's not happening," Whil told me. "And I agree with him. So far, you've only used your power to protect the pack, and the power is growing slowly. I doubt you'll suddenly turn into a power hungry murderous monster, which means we have time to figure this out."

"You don't know that," I insisted.

I didn't want to hurt anyone. In fact, all my instincts were telling me I had to protect the pack. But that only made it more important for me to ensure I wasn't the one the pack needed protection from.

"Audrey," Whil said as she rose and moved to sit on the couch beside me, her expression softening. "Yes, the power is growing inside you, but it's not woven into your soul. It might feel like it, but it's not. Your mate bonds are protecting you. Which means you might have access to that magic, but it's not influencing you."

Except I could hear the "not yet" at the end of her sentence.

KNOX

THE UNEVEN COBBLESTONE ALLEYWAYS OF ANAKAR TWISTED and turned, thankfully casting deep shadows in the bright midmorning light as Deacon and I in our wolf forms crept toward the heart of Anakar.

As much as it would have been better to sneak around at night, I wasn't dumb enough to risk being caught by the malicious spirits that appeared after sundown.

It was bad enough we could already smell more than a dozen humans, but these humans controlled an unknown number of grimalkins, not to mention had lightning weapons. I didn't want to add evil manifestations of Tzanagoth's power to the mix, so nighttime reconnaissance was out.

Just like every time I crossed onto the land affected by the sleeping malicious god, an ominous power pressed against my senses, making the fur at the back of my neck rise.

Fuck, I hated being in Anakar, and the last time we'd been here snake shadow monsters had exploded from the ground and tried to rip Audrey apart.

All because she'd tried to stand up against the asshole who'd tried to sacrifice her to a monster.

A growl bubbled in my throat. I wanted to tear Sterling apart and piss on his corpse, but the rip between realms wasn't big enough for me to get to Audrey's realm. Of course, that also meant it wasn't big enough for him to get to her, and I was just going to have to be grateful that there was one less threat out there to hurt Audrey.

They've gone down the left passage, Deacon said in my head as he sniffed the ground.

We'd been following the scents from the humans and the foul reek of their grimalkins, keeping to side streets and alleys to avoid detection. I'd hoped the merchants had picked someplace near the outskirts of the complex, but no, every turn drew us closer and closer to Tzanagoth's temple.

I don't like that they're so close to the god's power, I growled back at him.

Some of the myths say that the grimalkins were born from Tzanagoth's magic, Deacon replied. *Maybe they found something here that controls them.*

Sisters, I hoped not. If the merchants could figure out how to turn the grimalkins into weapons, then anyone could. Even if we bought the merchants' lightning weapons our pack would still be in danger. The weapons had a recharging time and wouldn't be able to take out a large pack before the beasts could attack.

We slunk out of the shadows to the wider intersection and hurried after the humans' scent just as the sounds of voices and footsteps came from the road ahead of us.

Shit. We had to get past a long row of buildings before we could slip into a parallel alley.

My gaze leaped from one crumbling structure to the next. Most of the entranceways had collapsed, but enough of the walls still stood that it would be a risk trying to jump over without making a sound — especially since there wasn't a lot of room to move around.

Then I caught sight of a hole where one building had fallen against its neighbor.

In here, I commanded, jerking my nose at the opening.

It was going to be a tight fit, but we only had a few seconds left and no other options.

The voices and steps were coming closer, and the humans were about to walk around the large tree and rubble covering three quarters of the path at the end of the road and see us.

Deacon dove for the hole, shifting to his human form before he reached it, and half slid half squirmed inside. I leaped after him, shifting as well. My wolf was easily twice the size of my human, and if Deacon's human had trouble getting in, it would be impossible for my wolf.

I shoved my head through but my shoulder hit the edge of the still-standing wall.

Shit shit shit.

I needed to get smaller, somehow. If I could get my shoulders through, the rest of me would get through.

Go sideways, Deacon said, grabbing my shoulders, wrenching me onto my side, and hauling me into the cool darkness.

"Did you hear something?" a man asked, his voice pitched a little too high as if he were afraid.

We froze, not risking going farther down the narrow alley we'd crawled into. The slightest move could knock loose the precarious pile of bricks around us. Even just a pebble breaking free could give us away.

"It's just rats," someone else laughed as the footsteps drew closer. "Stop jumping at everything. Raddix said we're protected from Tzanagoth's spirits."

"So *he* says," the first man shot back.

"Jeez," another man said, his voice low and gravelly, and three sets of legs stopped on the road in front of the hole we'd snuck through. "We've been here for over two weeks and nothing's happened."

"Lots has happened. Those spirits scream all night long," Afraid Guy said.

"But they haven't entered our camp," Gravelly Voice shot back. "And it's the middle of the day. There aren't any spirits around. Come on."

"So *you* say," Afraid Guy grumbled as the group walked away.

I glanced at Deacon. Yeah, he'd heard that, too. Raddix, whoever he was, had a way to keep his camp safe from the spirits, which meant someone had found some water or plants or stone or something that could control Tzanagoth's spirits.

Come on, I growled in Deacon's head as I squeezed out from the rubble into the alley and shifted back to my wolf. *Let's find their camp and get the fuck out of here.*

Deacon followed and shifted as well, and we crept in the direction the men had come from.

A few minutes later, we turned onto a short road that ended in brilliant sunlight, and beyond stood Tzanagoth's temple, the only structure in Anakar that hadn't crumbled with age.

My insides churned, an uneasiness settling in my limbs, and I drew close enough to see into the courtyard.

The courtyard was empty with the dry fountain and the monstrous statue of Tzanagoth about to eat his sacrifices standing in the center.

I was about to turn away when something shimmered at the corner of my eye and my pulse stalled.

No. Please no.

I dragged my attention toward the shimmer. It was back and, from the sight of the mangled corpse on the ground in front of it, someone had used a blood sacrifice to open— No, not one sacrifice there were two heads... except there weren't enough body parts for two people.

A growl bubbled in my throat. The man who'd tormented my mate, even tormenting her in her dreams, was back, and if he was powerful enough to open a rip between the realms, I had no doubt he'd actually come to our realm.

I wasn't sure if I could take him out. But I would. I had to.

Because that was the only way to protect Audrey.

AUDREY

I woke with a start, suddenly furious and completely confused. It must have been another dream, one I didn't remember. Except the second I thought that, I realized the anger was coming from my mating bonds.

Knox was back and he was pissed... except underneath all of that was a churning fear.

"What's wrong?" Bishop asked, his arms around me tightening and his body tense.

When I'd gone to bed, Bishop had still been at the fancy dinner in the ballroom. I'd tried to smile and nod — while also pretending to not understand anyone who used a translator — but it had been hard to focus.

Both Bishop and Whil — and even Cyrus once he'd found out about the dark magic inside me — had assured me I wasn't going to just snap and turn into a murderous maniac, but that didn't ease my fear.

I didn't want to control evil magic. I wanted nothing

to do with it. It was still getting stronger inside me and I didn't want to risk it infecting my soul bonds.

And a small part of me was terrified that all the progress I'd made in becoming stronger and recognizing that I did have value was because of the magic. Was the wildness inside me really my wolf awakening or was it the dark magic?

"Audrey," Bishop said, yanking me from my worries. "What's wrong?"

"Knox is back and he's angry."

Bishop frowned then closed his eyes. "Your bond is really strong. I can barely sense him, which means he's still a good five-minute run from Stonehaven." Then he threw back the blankets and sat up. "If he's pissed, he found something in Anakar. Let's go."

I hurried to my wardrobe and pulled out a shirt and pair of pants while Bishop grabbed his clothes draped over the back of the chair in the corner. We quickly got dressed and rushed out of the French doors in my sitting room.

Once again, I was up and it was barely dawn.

"Where are we going?" I asked, surprised that we'd stepped outside instead of staying in the Residence. I'd assumed Bishop would have gone to Cyrus's room to wake him.

"Whil's," Bishop replied, taking my hand.

I glanced up at the two moons still visible in the sky. "She's going to love that."

"If the merchants have a way of controlling the

grimalkins, then we're going to want her involved in the planning," he replied, his gaze going unfocused for a second.

"Cyrus is up. He's going to meet us. Now, come on," he said. "We need to keep our pace leisurely so no one knows something is going on."

My heart pounded as we strolled through the gardens toward Whil's greenhouse library cottage. Knox's anger roiled inside me and my wildness started to rise. I needed to move faster, take action, do something even if I knew that there was nothing we could do until Knox and Deacon got back to the Residence.

And even then, I wouldn't be able to do anything because I was wea—

I stopped myself before I could continue that thought. I wouldn't be able to do anything *right now* anyway, even if my mates and Cyrus would let me.

We reached Whil's cottage as Cyrus did and headed around to the side toward the greenhouse entrance while Cyrus banged on the front door.

"How long until Knox gets here?" I asked, struggling to block off some of Knox's anger.

I pushed as much love and support as possible through our bond as I fought to stay calm. Freaking out wouldn't help the situation, and if I was going to help, I needed to look strong and confident.

"He and Deacon are about two minutes out," Bishop replied as he led me through the greenhouse to the mismatched seating area at the back.

Cyrus met us there, and a moment later Whil entered from the cottage part of her house carrying a tray with a teapot and six cups. She set the tray on the table between us, pressed her hands against the pot, and closed her eyes. Golden light flashed around her hands and steam rose from the spout and around the edges of the lid.

Cyrus raised a surprised eyebrow before sitting in the cushioned armchair.

"I figured no one wanted to wait for the kettle to boil," Whil replied as she poured six cups of tea.

"You mean *you* didn't want to wait," Bishop corrected.

"It's not even dawn. Again," she huffed as she sat on the floor in the middle of three piles of books. "If this is what Cyrus thinks it is, I'm going to want tea."

It is, Knox replied in my head, stepping around a leafy plant with Deacon right behind him. *The merchants have set up camp*— "in Anakar and have over four dozen grimalkins," Knox finished, shifting into his human form halfway through.

He lifted me off the couch and took my seat, placing me in his very naked lap.

A shiver of need — that was completely inappropriate — teased down my spine. Knox hummed low in his throat, and the anger in our bond eased as if he'd needed to hold me to get himself back under control even though it hadn't felt as if he were on the verge of going feral.

"Fuck," Cyrus hissed.

"No shit," Deacon added. "We didn't stick around

long, but we counted about two dozen swordsmen and all those beasts."

"The rip between the realms is also back," Knox growled, his grip around me tightening. "It's not wide enough for a person to come through, but it might have been at some point. There were the remains of two bodies near it."

My desire turned cold and visions of last night's dream rushed through me. Except it hadn't really felt like a dream, and now I was willing to bet everything that it hadn't been.

Sterling had sacrificed Mila and Porter to open the rip and if their bodies were still there, then the rip had been large enough for them to have passed through. If it hadn't been large enough, there wouldn't be any bodies, they'd have burned to ash before even hitting the ground.

"Sterling is here," I told them.

And he was more powerful than before.

I'd barely escaped his control when he'd tried to get me to walk into the rip and burn up. He'd only had ghostly ram horns then, but if my dream hadn't been a dream but me witnessing what Sterling was doing then he could now turn into that monster.

"We won't let him hurt you," Cyrus said, his alpha power washing over me not in a command but as a protective cocoon. "Ever."

AUDREY

MY WILDNESS ROSE UP IN RESPONSE TO CYRUS'S POWER, while desire spread low in my core.

Mine. He was mine, and *I* was going to protect *him*, protect all of my mates, and not the other way around.

Cyrus held my gaze, his eyes filled with determination and hunger, and it felt like the air was sucked out of the room. For a moment there was just us, captured in a whirling vortex of desire and need, and my soul ached for him.

We still hadn't had our talk, but if he was going to tell me he couldn't be my mate I was going to scream. He'd sent me heated, possessive glances yesterday when he thought I wasn't looking, and I'd had to grit my teeth to not reciprocate.

We belonged together.

And I refused to let him deny it.

That said, I also knew now wasn't the time to get into

it. Cyrus needed to remain focused on saving our pack and so did I. Our relationship could be worked out later.

"We don't know for certain if Sterling is around or if he's even involved with the merchants," Deacon said.

"And the merchants are our first priority," I added. Protecting the pack protected our mates.

"We need to inform the other leaders." Cyrus set his teacup on the table and stood.

"Can we trust them?" Whil asked. "Bishop told me that Speaker Jundar wants to buy the weapons."

"Only because he doesn't know the increased beast attacks are because of the merchants," Bishop replied. "He's honorable. He'll want to put a stop to this, too."

"What we don't want is to tip off the merchants." Cyrus shot me another fierce look with a possessive heat burning in his mossy green eyes then strode out of the greenhouse.

I bit back a groan and sank deeper into Knox's embrace.

"We need a plan to quietly capture the merchants here," Deacon said, his gaze going unfocused for a second. "Finn is on his way."

"Agreed," Bishop replied. "It would be best if the merchants didn't know we were coming."

My thoughts whirled. With that many grimalkins, not to mention the swordmen who also probably had access to those deadly lightning weapons, we were going to need an army.

How many fighters did the pack have left? We were

going to be making up the most of it since there wasn't time to call in any cavalry.

From the conversations I'd overheard during dinner last night, the merchants were getting frustrated. I didn't know if they'd figured out Cyrus had been stalling the talks for the previous day and half, but they'd certainly figured out something wasn't right.

The gryphons could get to Stonehaven the fastest even though they were the farthest away, but they still needed a whole day to send a messenger back to their pack then another day for their hunters to show up and that would mean the hunters wouldn't be rested if we then headed straight to Anakar.

Which meant, if we were going to deal with merchants now — and since they could release the grimalkins on us at any time, now was way better than later — it was up to our pack to stop them and we were going to need anyone in Stonehaven capable of fighting.

And that included me. Somehow, I'd killed two grimalkins in the last fight, but more importantly, I could control them... I hoped. In the very least, I was certain I could influence them.

"You're going to need me," I said.

"Absolutely not!" Bishop replied as Knox snarled.

"You've gotten lucky and killed a few grimalkins," Deacon added, "but this is going to be different. There's a chance it won't be one or two of them at a time."

"Which is why you'll need me." I sat up straighter, staying within Knox's grasp because I knew if I stepped away from him, his wolf would lose it. "I can control the grimalkins."

"You controlled two," Whil said as Deacon's eyes widened with surprise.

"What do you mean you controlled them?" Knox demanded.

I turned to meet his wolf-darkened eyes. "Why do you think those grimalkins ran away?"

Knox stared back and his emotions churned through our bond. He was angry and afraid and that mixed with confusion and self-recrimination probably because he hadn't thought to wonder what had really happened.

"Forty-eight is a lot more than two," Bishop said softly.

"It doesn't matter if I can't control all of them. Controlling some will help," I insisted. "Even if I can just get them to hesitate. That might be enough to save someone's life."

"No," Knox snarled, his power crashing over me.

"Yes," I snarled back, meeting his power and forcing it back, proving that I was the more dominant alpha — although it hadn't felt like Knox had used all of his power. "I'm not stupid. I'm not going to run into the middle of them."

"Audrey, please," Bishop whispered, a rush of terror racing through our bond. "We have to protect you."

"And I have to protect *you*."

I understood how he was feeling. My instincts were

freaking out over the thought of my mates facing off against forty-eight grimalkins.

"I don't understand this power, but I have it and I'm going to use it." I was going to save my mates with it before it could turn me into a monster.

The other leaders arrived and we worked out a plan. Today we were going to slowly send wolves, gryphons, and King Gower's men out of Stonehaven so the merchants weren't tipped off. No one wanted to risk the merchants having men around town watching for unusual activity. Jundar's and Pimryl's men would stay since they needed translators, which could be dangerous for everyone involved.

Jundar and Pimryl agreed that they'd lock themselves and their translators into the smaller meeting room for a "leaders only" meeting, and all leaders' aides would distract the merchants saying the alliance was working on a final decision. At noon, Finn would arrest the merchants — since Cyrus and Folmar were certain the merchants would become suspicious by then.

Whil said she could make a sleeping potion with a mix of magic and the sedative we'd gotten from Kelna. She'd then use her magic to swirl it around all the swordsmen while they ate lunch to ensure they were all put to sleep.

Everyone understood why Whil had to join the strike force.

And everyone questioned why I was going along.

"She's killed three grimalkins," Knox growled even

though I could feel how much he wanted me to stay safe in the Residence.

Cyrus glanced at me, asking me with a look if I wanted to tell the truth. I was sure he and my guys could tell the others I was going and that was that, but the truth would come out anyway and it was better if everyone was prepared.

"We've discovered Audrey's alpha power is special and she can use it to command the grimalkins," Cyrus said.

Jundar's, Gower's, and Pimryl's eyes widened in surprise while Folmar's narrowed. I could sense her alpha power even though she was a gryphon, but I didn't know if she could sense wolf shifters' powers. And if she could sense mine now, she'd think I was an utter weakling.

"I plan on sticking to the back and helping how I can," I told everyone. They were all bigger than me and trained warriors, and it was clear I didn't have any fight training at all.

"Then it's decided," Folmar said as she stood.

She and Knox left and the rest of us waited a few minutes. Gower left next then Jundar and a few more minutes after that, Bishop and I headed out of Whil's greenhouse.

Outside, the faint light of dawn peeked over the horizon, signaling the start of a new day, and despite my worries, only the soft birdsong and the gentle rustle of leaves disturbed the tranquil morning air. The sun had yet to rise, but there was already a pleasant warmth in the air that spoke of bright summer days ahead.

It was as if nothing had changed.

And yet everything had changed.

And more changes were on the horizon.

I had a growing darkness inside me that terrified me, and yet I knew I had to use it to save my mates and my pack. If I didn't, the merchants with their monsters would destroy them all.

AUDREY

WE HEADED OFF THE RESIDENCE'S GROUNDS WITHOUT stopping for breakfast or supplies. Knox was going to pack what we needed and meet us at the edge of town with rations, and it was better for us to be seen in Stonehaven early so the merchants would think Bishop was with the other leaders.

For the most part, the streets were quiet, but I could see lights on behind windows and smell bacon and pastries cooking, a sure sign that the town was waking up.

We walked out of Old Town into New Town, the buildings becoming less residential and more commercial, to the large, square hospital with its mismatched architecture. Again, we avoided the courtyard at the front and entered through a modest foyer with the reception desk and comfortable chairs.

A few people napped in the chairs, but there was no one at the desk. It had only been a few days since the grimalkin attack, a lot of people had gotten hurt, and I suspected the staff was still stretched thin. No doubt they'd rationed the healing elixirs for the worst cases and the humans. Nova wouldn't use them all just in case the grimalkins attacked again. Which was smart but meant a lot of people were still suffering.

We took the stairs to the second floor, pausing at the top, and Bishop squeezed my hand.

"Meet me in the garden outside after you've checked on Quinn and Zavier. And remember we still haven't caught that assassin."

A shiver rolled down my spine. That was the last thing we needed on top of everything else.

The memory of his attack shuddered through me. It had been awful feeling so helpless... except, I hadn't been. Bile had burned my throat and my stomach had heaved. Maybe the assailant hadn't run away because Bishop was going to kill him, but because I'd compelled him.

Which was ridiculous. That would mean he was connected to the grimalkins.

"Be careful." Bishop captured my lips in a quick kiss, his love and worry pouring through our mating bond.

"Always," I said, breathless.

He rolled his eyes at me.

Yeah, I hadn't been careful during the grimalkin attack and if I had to do it again, I wouldn't change a thing. We both knew careful went out the window the second someone needed saving.

Bishop headed to the nurses' station at the end of the hall, but I stopped halfway down at Zavier's room.

The door was open a crack and I peeked in. Zavier still lay on the bed in his wolf form and I couldn't tell if he'd moved or not. Shifters could heal some serious injuries, especially if they stayed in whatever form they were in instead of shifting and draining their life force, so if Zavier was still out of it, that wasn't good.

Quinn sat in the chair beside his bed, also asleep clutching Zavier's paw, her face pale and drawn. She'd told me she thought of Zavier like a brother, but there was something more between them, and it was obvious, probably to everyone else but them.

I pushed the door open a little more. Every fiber of my being wanted to reach out and comfort Quinn, to reassure her that everything would be okay. But the truth was, I didn't know.

I had a bad feeling about Anakar and a lot of people could die if we couldn't keep the grimalkins in their pens — and not just those going to fight the merchants. The grimalkins could attack the town again, and Zavier being Zavier would jump into trouble not because it was his job, but because that was the type of man he was.

And if I could keep him from danger— If I could keep *anyone* in the pack safe, I would.

A flicker of wildness whispered through my soul, adding to my determination that I couldn't hide and let everyone else deal with this situation.

I had the power — hopefully. I had to help.

I eased the door shut and forced myself to step away. They needed sleep more than I needed to know how they were doing.

And I needed to get out of the hospital and find some breathing room before I lost it. Every room I passed with the beds filled with injured people was a reminder of the attack.

I couldn't let it happen again.

Funny how just a little while ago, I would have thought I was powerless to do anything, that no one would listen to me or want my help.

And now I didn't care what they thought. My wildness was steadily growing with each step down the hall, each whimper and sob and pained expression I heard and saw.

I didn't think I'd ever felt so angry or so determined. This was my pack and the merchants had hurt them. Mine.

I stormed down the back stairs, shoved open the door at the bottom, and strode into the garden where I was supposed to meet Bishop.

Dozens of people looked up at the sound of the door crashing open, and all eyes locked on me.

Shit.

I didn't want anyone to see me like this, but with the influx of patients, I should have known the hospital garden wouldn't be empty.

I sucked in a sharp breath, determined to will my wildness away. I couldn't do anything about anything right this moment and I needed to look calm.

I also needed to ignore my first instinct to hide from all those eyes along with my fury that hiding was my first instinct.

"Alpha," a tall woman in scrubs said. "I heard you saved the children in the smithy."

My gaze darted around the garden for an escape route while my wildness flared, enraged that I couldn't even control my body.

"Yes," I replied quietly, forcing a tight smile that I hoped conveyed some semblance of strength. "But Jaxon and Finn were there, too."

"I heard you killed a grimalkin," the woman said.

"I heard she killed two," a tired looking man added.

"I heard it was all a lie." Velora's sharp voice cut through the voices of the crowd and everyone fell silent.

The crowd in front of me parted and stepped back, and Velora strolled toward me.

"Everything about you is a lie," she added with a smirk. "I heard you used magic to trick Knox and Bishop into mating with you."

A few people gasped at her words, and a few others hardened their expressions, and everyone else looked upset at Velora. People might have believed her before the grimalkin attack, but even Finn, who'd once agreed with Velora, was supporting me now. No doubt he, along with the children, were talking about how I killed two grimalkins without even shifting.

"Now you're lying about killing grimalkins." She

glanced at the crowd. "How could a shifter who's so weak kill a grimalkin?"

My insides twisted, her tone too much like Merrick's when his question was a trap. How could I convince anyone that I'd killed those beasts when everyone could tell I was powerless?

Except I'd killed one, even before my alpha power started to manifest. I'd accidentally killed that grimalkin in Kelna when we're traveling north to break my bond with Knox.

"I challenge you," Velora yelled loud enough that people a block over could probably hear her. "You're a liar and a manipulator. Bishop was supposed to be my mate and you stole him from me. I'm taking him back."

Her claws extended from her fingertips and a soft thump of alpha power hit me. It caught me off guard, forcing me to take a step back, and Velora's sneer deepened.

My pulse thudded. I didn't know this pack's rules for a formal challenge. In my old pack, a challenge was to the death. But if I died, Bishop would die or go crazy.

"Bishop and I have already sealed our mate bond. You can't get rid of me or break us apart."

"Doesn't matter," Velora snarled. "I'm going to tear you up, make you so hideous he'll never be able to look at you again. Then he'll have to take a second mate. He'll make me his alpha mate."

"If you hurt me, Bishop won't love you. He'll hate you."

"He'll finally be able to see the truth!" A manic gleam flashed in her eyes. "Your spell will be broken and Bishop will love me. He'll never look at you again and I'll lock you away to be forgotten. You're weak and pathetic. An alpha shouldn't even bother looking at you let alone one like Bishop."

"Velora—"

"Remember your place and respect me," she screeched. "I'm going to be your alpha. I deserve to be alpha."

My wildness surged, my power thudding hard within my chest.

"Deserve?" I snarled. "You don't deserve anything."

The woman was completely insane. I didn't know how Cyrus or Bishop hadn't seen it. I was sure they'd been aware of Velora's crush, but I had no idea how she'd managed to keep this level of crazy hidden for so long.

And that pissed me off.

She didn't deserve to be alpha and she sure as hell didn't deserve my mate. She wasn't going anywhere near Bishop and I'd be damned if she had any influence over this pack. I'd already lived in a pack with a cruel dictator. I'd never let the people of this pack live with an insane one.

"Being alpha isn't something to be won or deserved," I said, my voice low, dangerous. "It shouldn't be something the strong take because they can or because they want power over others. It's something to be earned. It's an act of full submission to serving the pack."

"An alpha never submits," Velora screamed at me, her power rolling over me in a weak demand to kneel before her.

I squared my shoulders and let her power hit me. She didn't have a strong alpha power and only a few of the bystanders sagged to their knees.

"Why aren't you kneeling?" she demanded, jerking forward a step as if drawing closer to me would make her power stronger.

But she was nothing compared to Cyrus. Hell, half of the people watching this *challenge* were stronger than her.

"Kneel!" she roared, with another weak slap.

"You kneel," I roared back, and my wildness let loose. My power surged from my body, slamming over her and everyone in the garden.

She gasped and dropped to her knees, her eyes wide with shock, along with everyone else.

"I'm not weak and pathetic," I told her, fighting to hold my power back so as not to flatten her like the wildness inside me wanted. "And even if I wasn't an alpha, I wouldn't be weak. My strength comes from my compassion and my determination to protect. I'll never let you take my place. I'll never let a selfish, cruel alpha lead my pack, because it's *my* pack. Mine. Bishop and Knox. They're mine."

A wave of power slipped my grip and slammed into Velora, forcing her to press her forehead against the ground, her power weakly fluttering against mine, unable to even compete.

"This whole pack is mine," I growled. "Mine to serve and protect like an alpha is supposed to. Do you understand me?"

Velora groaned and twisted her head the fraction of an inch necessary to glare up at me with one eye.

"Do. You. Understand?"

BISHOP

I stood at the hospital's back door, the cool metal handle pressing into my palm and my eyes fixed on the garden. Power poured from Audrey in great waves, crashing over me and making my knees weak, while everyone else in the garden knelt in submission.

But they were just the bystanders caught up in Audrey's power. Her real target was Velora who lay prostrate on the ground, her head turned just enough so she could glare at Audrey.

"Do. You. Understand?" Audrey snarled, sounding more like Knox than the quiet, shy girl we'd pulled out of the river.

Sisters, she was amazing.

I knew she had a warrior's spirit and now others knew it as well. She wasn't some weakling they could push around and they shouldn't think that because she didn't exude alpha power that they could say and do whatever they wanted with her.

Pride swelled within me and I let it pour through our mating bond. Audrey had come so far from the frightened woman who had been abused by her previous pack alpha.

She'd been forced into silence and invisibility by her previous pack, conditioned to fear speaking up or even being seen, and I had no doubt standing up to Velora made Audrey uncomfortable. I didn't think she'd ever want to draw attention to herself.

And yet, here she was, asserting herself as my mate and claiming her position as alpha.

"Do you?" Audrey pressed, more of her power crashing down on Velora and washing over everyone else.

"Yes," Velora hissed, her words soft but still audible.

Audrey huffed. "I didn't hear you."

"Yes, *alpha*," Velora said, louder this time.

Audrey's power eased, releasing everyone from their submissive position.

I mentally reached out to Harlow. She was an older watchman who should have retired a few years ago and Finn had assigned her to the hospital. With the fear and heightened emotions from the attack, Cyrus and I thought it best if there was someone who could deal with any conflict.

Harlow, I said in her mind. *Meet me in the hospital garden. You need to make an arrest.*

Of course, she replied, and I opened the back door and joined Audrey.

Velora's eyes flashed bright, her hope clear that I'd take her side or that she'd be able to convince me Audrey was dangerous. But I scowled at her. I'd heard everything. She'd threatened to permanently maim my mate and that was unforgivable.

I glanced at everyone else, worried that someone would side with Velora, but most of them looked awed and proud of Audrey. Those who weren't appeared shocked by the display of power they'd just witnessed.

And I couldn't blame them. Audrey didn't radiate any alpha power until it broke through the curse containing it and exploded around her. After, the curse took over again, and she was back to looking like the weakest shifter in existence.

It shouldn't have taken releasing her power to convince everyone she was exactly where she belonged, but it still warmed my heart to see that nobody seemed upset or angry with Audrey for asserting her dominance.

Instead, their eyes held contempt for Velora. Her true, horrible nature had been exposed, and with this revelation, any credibility she had in spreading those nasty rumors about Audrey was now in tatters.

"Velora," I said, struggling to keep my voice even.

My wolf wanted to rip her to pieces for even thinking about doing those things to Audrey, but I couldn't risk looking like I wasn't in control. That would diminish Audrey's strength in standing up for herself, making it look like she needed my protection when she didn't — at least not in this situation.

"Audrey is my fated mate. There won't ever be another woman for me and I knew it the moment I saw her." I glanced at Audrey and offered her a soft smile while sending all my love to her through our bond. "We're destined to be together."

Audrey's love raced back to me in response and the adoration in her expression stole my breath. I'd never tire of seeing that look or feeling her love, and I'd thank the Sisters for the rest of my life that they blessed me with such an incredible mate.

Then Audrey's expression hardened and she turned to Velora.

"I never wanted to be alpha and I still don't. But if it means I can protect this pack, so be it. I don't want to issue commands. That's Cyrus, Bishop, and Knox's job, but in this situation I will," Audrey said. "I strip you of your rank of beta."

"You can't do that!" Velora snapped.

A ripple of Audrey's power swept through the garden. "I think I've proven that I can."

"Bishop—" Velora looked at me with pleading eyes and I placed my hand against the small of Audrey's back.

"I stand by my mate," I said.

"So do I," someone in the crowd mumbled. "Velora is crazy."

Velora jerked around to see who'd spoken, her

expression contorted with anger and humiliation. "Who said that? Who dares say that about me."

The back door opened and Harlow strode out. I acknowledged her with a nod, and before I could even tell her what was going on, she assessed the situation and moved to apprehend Velora without hesitation.

When I heard Velora talking trash about your mate, I figured this day would come, she said in my head.

You should have said something, I replied.

The grimalkins attacked and it slipped my mind. I'm sorry, alpha.

Understandable. A lot had happened in the last couple of days, so I couldn't blame her for not coming to me with a worry. All she'd had was a conversation, not any proof that Velora was actually going to do something to Audrey. Even Cyrus, Knox, and I had been worried about Velora but hadn't done anything to prevent this confrontation.

I sighed as Harlow dragged Velora away. Despite my wolf's fury that Velora had threatened our mate, I couldn't help but feel a twinge of sadness for Velora. I'd known she'd been trying to get me to date her and had softly turned her down, but I hadn't known she'd been consumed by ambition and jealousy. If I'd been firmer in my rejection early on, maybe it wouldn't have turned out this way.

But I knew, deep in my soul, that was just wishful thinking. Velora had always been on the path of self-destruction and had done a good job at hiding all the ugly parts of herself.

"Come on," I said, nudging Audrey into movement and leading her out of the garden toward the market.

She leaned close, bumping her shoulder against mine and our fingers brushed. Desire zapped up my arm at the slight contact, and I took her hand in mine, entwining our fingers together. My heart swelled with pride and love for this incredible woman, and I swore I'd do everything in my power to protect her... even if she did want to walk to the heart of Anakar and help us defeat forty-eight grimalkins.

We leisurely strolled down Main Street to the market, even as my insides churned with the urge to hurry, do something, start saving my pack. Audrey's own impatience bled through the bond, fueling mine and making my wolf strain against my control.

I shoved him back down, reminding him we had a part to play. The merchants could have spies in the city, and if our plan to attack their camp was going to work, we needed the element of surprise.

But damn it. It was hard to concentrate with Audrey's emotions fueling mine.

"Audrey," I murmured to her. "Take a breath. We need to act natural."

"Right." She sucked in a deep breath and released it, some of her tension draining from our mating bond.

After that, I flirted with her, trying to distract her from what was coming. Seeing her blush and smile, so sweet and beautiful, made me fall in love with her all over again.

We reached the market, and Audrey and I strolled along the main paths, taking note of the damage and the progress of the rebuilding efforts while exchanging pleasantries and words of encouragement with those hard at work.

"I can't wait to see this place bustling again," Audrey said brightly to the owner of the bookstore we'd paused at the first time I'd taken Audrey here. I could feel her genuine hopefulness mixed with the urgency to hurry up and protect my pack.

"Thank you, alpha," he replied, and a thread of discomfort slipped down our bond.

"Audrey, please," she murmured.

The bookstore owner hummed and nodded but didn't agree to Audrey's request, and we strolled farther down the street.

"I'm never going to get used to that," she said. "They don't constantly call you alpha."

"They'll stop saying it soon," I chuckled. "They just want to show their respect. You did an amazing thing saving those children. The whole pack is grateful."

Finally, we reached the edge of town and quickly slipped between two still-standing shops and out into the grasslands beyond.

The tall grasses stretched in front of us, the land rolling with rises and dips. The goal was to head north, getting closer to the pack's full-sized sacred grove — not the private one on the Residence's ground — then head east so it wasn't so obvious that there were wolves running away from Stonehaven.

I led Audrey down a hill and away from town to where Knox waited for us.

He sat in the grass in his naked human form — something he'd been spending more and more time in since mating with Audrey — with a single backpack containing emergency supplies and— was that long black pole in the grass a fence post?

Joy flooded our twin bond. It wasn't nearly as strong as the emotions between me and Audrey, but it was still noticeable, and I was amazed at how Audrey had turned his life around.

Before she'd crashed into our lives, he'd been withdrawn, and I had feared he was slipping beyond my reach and on the verge of permanently going feral.

We'd only recently gotten him back and I hadn't wanted to lose him again. He was my twin. The other half of my soul, just like Audrey was our souls' match.

"Here," he said, picking up the fence post and offering it to Audrey.

Love flooded our bond and she gave him a heart-stopping smile.

"I had one of Jaxon's apprentices sharpen the end into a proper point," he said gruffly, a hint of blush coloring his cheeks. "Just in case."

I didn't want Audrey to be forced to defend herself. Just thinking of her in harm's way made my wolf rage and I knew Knox felt the same.

But neither of us could deny we needed her in Anakar. Hell, even Cyrus had caved, knowing that if she could control the grimalkins even just a little bit, she could save lives.

Which meant Knox was right. If our mate who couldn't shift was going to fight with us, she needed a weapon.

AUDREY

I ACCEPTED THE SPEAR FROM KNOX WHILE BISHOP TOOK off his clothes and put them in the pack. The wildness inside me pulsed stronger, part in desire at the sight of Bishop and Knox's powerful naked bodies, and part in determination, and I wrapped its strength around me while praying it wouldn't fail me when I really needed it.

So far it had always been there when I needed it, but I didn't have any control over it.

"Let's go," Bishop said, taking a step away from the town and shifting into his large black wolf. I'd seen a shifter shift many times before and still the action seemed fluid and beautiful... and heartbreaking.

I shoved back my disappointment as soon as it flickered to life. I didn't want my mates to feel it. I was happy with my life right now — with the exception of the chaos the merchants and their grimalkins had created. I didn't need to be able to shift.

And yet that broken part of me that still hadn't completely healed ached.

I was incomplete.

Sure, I had alpha power now when I really needed it... maybe... hopefully, but that could be because of the dark magic growing inside me.

My true wolf nature was still imprisoned by my ancestral curse, and there was no way of knowing if my wolf would ever fully awaken.

And I could deal with my insecurities later. I was stronger than I'd ever been before and I had mates who supported me.

My thoughts lurched to Cyrus as I secured the pack over my shoulders and Knox shifted and knelt so I could climb onto his back.

Cyrus was mine and I wasn't going to accept anything less than his bond. My soul and wildness wouldn't let me, and they sure as hell didn't care that he'd hurt me. To them, he'd apologized and treated me with the kindness and respect I deserved. It might have been awkward between us going to the healing pools and coming back, but I couldn't deny that he'd stopped pushing me away.

He also listened to me more and considered my suggestions, even asked for them. I didn't know what was holding him back, especially with the hunger in his gaze every time he looked at me, but I wouldn't accept any more excuses.

I might not have formed a bond with him when we

had sex like I had with Bishop, but I knew in the depths of my being that he was the final piece of my destiny.

Bishop took off and Knox followed, the guys slowly increasing their speed to an easy run so I had time to adjust since I only had one hand to hold onto him.

The grasslands stretched before us, a sea of rippling yellow-green rolling hills with the dark splotch of Darkweald in the distance, and the wind whipped at my face and tugged at my hair. The day was turning into the perfect summer's day without a cloud in the sky, but it wasn't enough to distract me from my worries.

It was late afternoon when we reached the campsite, my stomach growling its complaint over skipping breakfast and lunch. It was going to be unimpressed with rations for dinner, but it couldn't be helped. We were trying to amass our warriors in secret. Fires, tents, or even too-loud conversations could give us away even though we were still half a day away from the heart of Anakar.

And we could *not* be discovered. There were a lot of grimalkins — possibly too many for our small force to handle — but the merchants also had their devastating lightning weapons, and I had no doubt some of the weapons were with their swordsmen in Anakar.

It would have been great if we could have attacked them while they slept. We'd have still needed to be sneaky, but darkness and fewer people wandering around lessened the chance we'd be caught. But no one wanted to risk attracting the attention of Tzanagoth's malicious spirits, which were more powerful and active at night.

Which meant Cyrus decided camp was near the river and about twenty feet from the forest with its perpetual mist and ominous power. Knox and Deacon hadn't had time to confirm everywhere the merchant's swordsmen went and we just had to pray they didn't come to this side of the forest.

I slid off Knox's back as Cyrus approached, his gaze capturing mine, reaching into my soul and connecting to the part of me that knew he was mine, before sliding to the fence post-turned-spear in my hands.

"Good idea," he said with a brisk nod. "Grab something to eat. We're just waiting on a few more people."

Our remaining fighters arrived just as the sun was setting. I'd eaten as many tough dried rations as I could and settled on the ground in Bishop's arms with a blanket wrapped around me.

Knox, in his wolf form, lay beside us, his head on his paws, his eyes darting from person to person, on guard. A churning uneasiness rolled through the bond, Knox's fear of being surrounded by too many people, and I pushed loved and confidence back to him because I could also feel his desire to stay with me and Bishop and not hide in the tall grass and deepening twilight.

When I'd first met Knox, he'd wanted nothing to do with me or anyone else except maybe his brothers. He could barely be inside for more than a couple of hours at most and he avoided everyone. He could only stand a small group of people who he was close to, everyone else was too much. And we now had over fifty people standing twenty feet away.

Knox huffed and leaned into me, his unease growing along with his determination to stay, as Cyrus urged everyone to come closer.

"We leave for Anakar at first light," he said, his voice hushed. "Two scout parties will go ahead of us and take out any swordsmen as we go, but I want everyone to keep their eyes open. We can't afford to lose the element of surprise."

Everyone murmured their agreement. Half of them had seen how destructive just a single blast from one of the merchants' lightning weapons could be, and the other half had heard about it. No one wanted to be on the receiving end.

"Our goal is to reach a secure location near the swordsmen's camp and the grimalkins' pens," Gower added. "There we split into three groups. The quick strike group, their immediate backup, and the rest of you, including the medics, in case everything goes sideways."

"We're hoping the everyone-else-group gets bored," Folmar said.

"Better to show up and do nothing than not be there when needed," Deacon said, and the men and women around us nodded in agreement.

And that something was the grimalkins escaping their pens and the merchants being able to use their lightning weapons on us.

The thought sent a shudder of fear rushing through me and Bishop tightened his grip around me.

But with every beat of my heart, my determination grew. I'd protect my mates and my pack at all costs.

As we continued discussing strategies, my thoughts kept drifting to my own role in this battle. I had to hold the grimalkins in place long enough for the others to kill them, but what if I wasn't strong enough?

The fear gnawed at me, but I pushed it down, determined to do my part and protect my friends even as another worry surfaced in my mind: Sterling.

If he truly was in this realm, what would that mean for all of us? He was ruthless and power-hungry, a threat to everyone I held dear.

Except I couldn't let fear control me. I'd faced Velora and put her in her place. I could do the same with Sterling.

I had to.

But first we had to take care of the merchants and protect the pack.

Cyrus woke me just before dawn the next morning with a gentle touch on my shoulder. Slowly, I opened my eyes and was captured in his dark mossy green gaze.

For a second, time stood still between us, and my breath caught in my throat. His power stuttered against mine, as if he couldn't fully control it when he looked at me, but from the yearning in his eyes, I knew it wasn't because he was upset at me.

Heat rose from my core, aching for him to hold me,

kiss me, claim me like he had in the shower room in the hospital. But then his alpha-in-charge mask fell into place and he gave me a tight nod.

He wasn't going to address whatever lay between us. Not now. And while I understood his reasons — everyone in the pack was counting on him to lead this mission to success — my wildness wanted to cement her claim on him. He was mine, and I didn't want anything to happen to him before I'd made that perfectly clear to him and everyone else.

"Quick breakfast, then we head out." He jerked his head, indicating I should wake Bishop, who I was half lying on, and went to rouse the few others who were still asleep.

I groaned and stretched. My body was stiff from sleeping on the ground — well, half on the ground — and I pressed my nose against Bishop's neck, breathing in his bright fresh-cut grass sent while savoring the heat radiating from Knox's wolf pressed tight against my back.

Today was the day we stopped future grimalkin attacks or the day I lost my mates because Bishop, Knox, and Cyrus wouldn't give up. They'd give their lives to protect their pack. And I would too.

We ate more rations for breakfast before crossing the threshold into Darkweald and picking our way between the trees and underbrush, risking running into spirits by straying off the trail to avoid detection.

Knox and seven other hunters shifted into their wolves and prowled around and ahead of us, watching for danger while the rest of us walked as quickly and quietly as we could.

Mist and darkness shrouded the forest, chilling my skin, and the heavy, ominous power I'd felt every time I'd been in Darkweald pressed against my senses.

The evil magic unfurled inside me, a small, insidious darkness that twisted in my stomach. It called to the ominous power pressing down on me, and a mix of fear and relief flickered through me, drawing Bishop's attention.

"I just got confirmation where my—" I glanced at the shifters in front of me. They were close enough to hear me even if I whispered and I didn't want them to think I was a monster — even if I was terrified that I was going to become one.

I pressed a hand over my heart and Bishop nodded his understanding.

Knowing will help Whil figure out how to deal with it, he said in my head. *But you need to focus on right here and now. Don't let this distract you.*

Now it was my turn to nod, and I turned my attention back to the mist and the partially visible trees and under-brush. Cyrus was taking a huge risk in letting me come along, especially if I couldn't get my unwanted magic to control the grimalkins, but I refused to be a burden. I'd promised I'd be helpful, that I'd control the grimalkins, and I would. I had to.

By mid-morning we reached the remains of a stone building with trees, weeds, and tall grass growing around the rubble of the fallen walls and bursting through what was left of the tiled floor.

From there, we moved silently between the decaying buildings, our senses on high alert for any sign of danger even with our scouts searching for trouble ahead of us.

The air was thick with tension and nervous alpha power. No one wanted to face all those grimalkins let alone the swordsmen with lightning weapons, but we were all going to do it if we had to.

Please, God, don't let us have to.

Just before noon, we arrived at our primary defensive position. The building wasn't very big, probably a thirty by twenty rectangle, and lacked a roof, but all four walls looked solid and sturdy. Collapsed buildings on either side of the structure blocked the windows, leaving only the front and back doors as entry points.

If we had to make our stand here, we wouldn't be able to hold out for long against the lightning weapons, but the confining doorways would force the grimalkins to attack one at a time.

That, however, was only if our plan didn't work.

Please, God, gods, Sisters, anyone. Let it work.

CYRUS

A WEIGHT SQUEEZED MY CHEST AND I FOUGHT TO KEEP MY expression strong and stoic. I'd never been so fearful before a fight in my life, and it had everything to do with the woman standing a few feet away, boxed in by my brothers, her mates.

I loved her so much my heart ached, but I couldn't bring myself to tell her she was meant to be my mate, that I'd known the truth the moment she'd woken in the Residence after we'd found her in the river.

Our plan to take down the merchants' swordsmen was a dangerous one, and I couldn't shake the thought of what would happen if something went wrong.

Sure, Knox and Bishop would look out for her, and she had the disturbing dark magic inside her to protect her against the grimalkins — if she could actually control more than two — but knowing that did little to ease my fears.

If push came to shove, she'd risk everything if she thought she could save someone, especially one of her mates.

Which was why I wasn't going to tell her how I felt until this fight was done.

Bishop might be insisting I tell her first, but if something happened to me, I couldn't bear the thought of breaking her heart... because like Audrey, I'd risk everything, even give my life, to protect her and my brothers.

My wolf heaved inside me and I tightened my hold on him. I couldn't afford to lose control. Precision and keeping calm were what I needed right now, not the ferocious fury of my beast.

"Alright, everyone, listen up," I said just loud enough to be heard. "The grimalkins' pens and the swordsmen's camp are close." I pointed in the camp's direction. "They're around the corner then thirty feet to a slightly wider area. The buildings are recessed from the other buildings, which is good for us. It'll give us cover."

"Does everyone remember their assignment?" Gower asked and everyone nodded while Bishop turned to Whil.

"Can you sense them?" he asked.

Whil closed her eyes, her perpetual golden glow brightening for a second. "There's twelve lightning weapons and they're all together, in the direction of the swordsmen's camp."

Perfect. I'd hoped that the merchants wouldn't have armed their swordsmen with deadly weapons and it looked like they hadn't. That didn't mean the swordsmen didn't have access to them, but they weren't carrying them around on patrol and we wouldn't need to keep up with our careful hunting once we'd secured the weapons.

"Alright, let's move," I commanded, and we split into our respective groups.

I led the strike and backup teams, creeping to the corner, our footsteps softly crunching over stone and forest debris.

We reached the corner, and I glanced down the street where the grimalkins' pens and the swordsmen's camp were.

All clear.

Time to do this.

I glanced back at Audrey, my heart aching with the need to protect her.

Please, Sisters. Keep her safe.

Bishop, who stood beside her, caught my gaze, his expression determined. He'd protect her. I knew he would. But the knowledge didn't ease my or my wolf's worries.

I turned back to our target, a pile of rubble thirty feet down the wide road just before the recess in the buildings.

With Knox in his wolf form padding silently beside me and the rest of the strike team following behind us, I carefully slunk down the street, keeping close to the buildings on the same side of the street as the pens.

I reached the rubble and glanced around the edge into the recess. The grimalkins' guard looked bored as he leaned against the open doorway to the building that held the grimalkins' pens.

The large building was just as Deacon had described and as solid as the one I'd chosen for our group's defensive position, which meant if we could take out the swordsmen, the grimalkins would stay contained.

Beside the building containing the grimalkins' pens sat a similarly sized structure. It was in worse condition, with its far corner crumbled almost to the ground, and the archways over the front windows collapsed, leaving only a jagged façade. The front wall, now a mix of fallen windows and uneven edges, ranged between four feet to seven feet high, and through the gaps, I could clearly see and hear the swordsmen sitting around a campfire, eating their lunch and chatting with each other, oblivious to the imminent threat.

Unfortunately, there weren't any nearby alleys, but I trusted Knox to take out the guard before he made a noise and alerted the other swordsmen.

He was the pack's best hunter for a reason, and we were going to need all his skill to pull this off.

Go, I told Knox, and he slipped past the rubble, his enormous black wolf somehow melting into the shadows cast by the ruined building and overgrown brush beside us, the noise from the swordsmen in their camp covering any sound he might have made.

He slunk with ease, getting closer and closer to the guard outside the grimalkins' pens.

My pulse pounded, and my wolf pressed against my control, wanting to let loose and fight.

Someone in the swordsmen's camp laughed louder than the others, drawing the guard's attention. Knox leaped forward and shifted into his human form at the last second. With one clawed hand, he sliced open the guard's throat, and with the other he clamped it over the guard's mouth.

Go, I told Whil, before Knox had even set the dead guard on the ground.

I hurried forward, Whil close on my heels, both of us trying to keep as low to the ground and as quiet as possible. The sound of the swordsmen talking would help if we were careful, but we still had to move fast. Someone could look our way or walk out the door at any second. We couldn't let the swordsmen grab the lightning weapons.

We reached the edge of the crumbling building.

Just a little closer, I told Whil. *We need to get to that lower portion closer to their campfire.*

It was only a few feet away, but even with her magic swirling the potion in the air, it was best to toss the potion as close to the men as possible.

She nodded and pulled the jar of potion from her bag, her hands shaking.

I motioned for Whil to go ahead of me, just as a swordsman stepped out of the entranceway.

His eyes widened in surprise and I leaped forward, extending my claws from my fingertips.

Throw the jar! I commanded.

The swordsman started to draw his sword, but I was faster, slashing my claws through his neck before the weapon was unsheathed.

Whil hurled the jar with all her strength, and it smashed against the ground, releasing a golden mist. Her summer fae glow flared bright and the mist whooshed around those inside.

The men dropped their lunches, scrambling to draw their weapons and attack us, while six of them ran for an open crate on the other side of a row of cots. That had to be where they were keeping the lightning weapons.

The swordsman closest to the doorway jabbed at me with his sword, but I dodged, stepping close to the man, and raked my claws through his stomach and chest.

A growl bubbled in my throat as my wolf surged to the surface, not to take over, but to ensure we had all the power and ferocity needed to protect what was ours.

A few feet away, a man rushed toward Whil, but Deacon was a step behind her. He pulled her out of the way of the man's blade before attacking back.

Folmar and Knox joined him, protecting Whil and keeping the men away from the grimalkins' pens. We just needed to keep them contained until Whil's potion could knock them out.

But as I thought that, two of the swordsmen shoved the cots aside and reached the crate.

Shit.

Folmar, I said. She was the only one who could get

past the group of men in front of us to stop the others from using the dangerous weapons.

On it. She leaped into the air, shifting into her majestic gryphon, and used her wings to sail over everyone's heads, landing on the crate and crushing it with her front paws.

The swordsman who'd thankfully hadn't been able to grab a weapon, lurched back with a yelp. He landed on his ass then kept on going, collapsing onto the shattered tiles.

The man beside him collapsed as well, then another and another. Whil's sleeping potion was finally taking effect.

Thank the Sisters.

I blew out a heavy breath, my chest heaving from exertion, and relief washed over me. One slight mishap not counted, everything had gone according to plan. A quick glance told me no one had gotten hurt and we hadn't needed all the extra fighters.

AUDREY

I EASED MY GRIP ON MY SPEAR AND RELEASED THE BREATH I'd been holding when all the swordsmen passed out — Bishop having led our team down the street to the edge of the recess once we'd heard fighting. None of the swordsmen had managed to fire a lightning weapon, and save for being spotted before Whil could throw the potion, everything had gone according to plan.

And yet...

Something didn't feel right.

The air was heavy with the ominous power that felt like it was slowly and steadily growing, and my stomach churned as the dark magic inside me pulsed.

I sucked in a deep breath, determined to ignore my aching belly and the chill settling in my bones.

Cyrus and Knox tied up the unconscious swordsmen, and Whil used her power to magically lock the lightning weapons, preventing anyone from using them, like all of the alliance leaders had agreed on.

Everyone was going to be safe.

Except the wildness inside me screamed that I needed to stay alert.

Something was going to happen. Something—

The ominous power flared, stealing my breath, and the front wall of the building holding the grimalkins' pens exploded.

Debris flew everywhere, and the snarling creatures raced out, half of them rushing into the swordsmen's camp toward Cyrus and the others while the rest stampeded toward my group.

A skin-crawling wave of the grimalkins' alpha power slammed into me along with their heavy foul stench, and the darkness inside me pounded faster. Red light flashed in the eyes of a large grimalkin and my pulse stalled.

The guys had said the grimalkin who'd recently attacked had been more aggressive and possibly smarter than those that had attacked before, and I'd never seen a grimalkin with red eyes.

Maybe I'd imagined it.

But the red flashed again in another grimalkin's eyes, reminding me of the snake monsters Sterling had summoned when he couldn't get me to walk into the rip between realms and kill myself.

And none of that mattered. I needed to harness the darkness inside me and control the monsters before they killed everyone I loved.

I rushed forward, not knowing if I could control the grimalkins in the swordsmen's camp from where I stood. The last time I'd controlled them, they'd been five feet from me, and right now I was at least fifty feet away from Cyrus and the others.

"Audrey." Bishop grabbed my wrist but I jerked free.

"I need to get closer."

"Pretty sure you're close enough," Gower snapped as he swung his sword at a grimalkin's head while two other wolves attacked the beast's haunches.

I jerked my attention away from the grimalkins attacking in the swordsmen's camp to the chaos all around me. Men and women from the backup fighters poured past us, joining the fight, while the medics hung back, waiting for a chance to get to the injured.

Grimalkins kept pouring from the building, and my pulse roared with fear, my breath too sharp and fast. I'd never seen so many of the beasts before, and while I knew Knox had reported that the merchants had over four dozen, it hadn't occurred to me how overwhelming that would look.

Could I even control that many?

Someone screamed and Bishop wrenched me out of the way of a grimalkin's claws.

I had to.

I mentally grasped at the darkness inside me, my stomach seizing with nausea, bile burning the back of my throat, and a ferocious rage bursting to life inside me along with my wildness.

Mine. This pack was mine. Bishop, Knox, and Cyrus were mine.

Mine mine mine.

Black smoke puffed from my mouth and burned across my tongue.

They were going to freeze and they were going to freeze now.

"Submit!" I screamed, releasing a skin-crawling wave of my own alpha power.

All the wolf shifters and gryphons stumbled as if I'd affected them, too, even when the gryphons shouldn't have been able to sense my alpha power, and all of the grimalkins froze.

For a second everyone was staring at me, but instead of cringing away — like I knew I would later — I squared my shoulders and raised my chin, riding the ferocity of my alpha power.

The dark magic heaved against my control and I gritted my teeth.

"Don't just stand there," I snarled. "Kill them."

Cyrus lunged at the grimalkin in front of him and tore his claws through its throat with a shocking spray of brilliant red blood. Next to him, Knox clamped his powerful jaws around another grimalkin's neck, killing it, while Folmar tore into another.

Smoke burned out my nostrils and my stomach heaved.

Hold on and don't puke. Please don't puke.

My grip on the darkness wavered and the ominous power pounded against my senses, straining my control.

The fighters took out ten more grimalkins and I squeezed my eyes shut. I could do this. I *was* doing it. I just... needed... a little more—

My darkness stuttered, suddenly weakening, and the magic slipped through my mental fingertips.

No. Please no.

A grimalkin roared and someone screamed. My eyes flew open to see the remaining grimalkins springing back into action.

Fuck fuck fuck.

I scrambled to regain control of the magic, but it kept stuttering, there and strong one minute, weak and thin the next.

"Alpha," someone yelled.

I wrenched my gaze around, searching for which of my mates was in danger, just in time to see a grimalkin lunge toward me. I was the alpha they were yelling at.

Both Bishop and Gower were busy fending off other grimalkins, there wasn't anywhere to run, and I couldn't count on the dark magic to save me.

With a scream, I wrenched my spear up to stab it, even while desperately trying to seize control of it. But I couldn't grasp the magic, and it heaved its head aside, sending my spear tip scraping against its tough hide.

Shit.

I jerked my spear toward it again as Bishop slammed all of his claws in the beast's haunches and, with a strength I hadn't thought possible even for a shifter, tossed the grimalkin away from me.

"Stay back," he snarled at me, his eyes completely dark, his wolf controlling his body. Then he leaped toward the next closes grimalkin and swiped at it.

Ahead of him, Folmar screamed Whil's name, her voice sliced through the chaos and I wrenched my attention to see her tearing into a grimalkin with her sharp beak and claws, defending Whil from the snarling creature, but there were more surrounding them.

With a roar, Deacon swooped in, grabbed Whil and threw her over his shoulder. He bolted toward me, dodging grimalkin claws and teeth, but one grimalkin was faster than him, raking its sharp claws through his shoulder.

He stumbled and the grimalkin's back legs bunched, ready to pounce.

"No," I screamed, the darkness inside me surging.

I threw out my hand as if that would stop them... and it did. All the grimalkins froze again.

Yes!

But before anyone could kill them, the ground beneath us exploded, and the horrible black flying snake monsters erupted from the earth. Their shark-like teeth snapped hungrily and their red eyes glowed with malevolent intent.

No, oh fuck no.

"Are you fucking kidding me?" Bishop snarled as he

killed the frozen grimalkin in front of him then lunged for another.

"Kill the grimalkins first," Cyrus commanded over the yells and screams and hisses filling the air.

The anger inside me blazed hotter, and I tightened my grip on the darkness inside me, determined to keep the grimalkins from fighting.

We were *not* going to lose this fight. We had to kill all of the grimalkins, especially if they weren't as natural as they were supposed to be.

Snakes swarmed around us, tearing bloody chunks out of men, wolves, and gryphons alike. Bishop yanked a snake off his biceps, its many teeth tearing through his flesh, before wrenching away a snake wrapped around Gower's neck, strangling him.

The ominous force pounded stronger and stronger against my senses, making the darkness inside me surge, and half a dozen snakes closest to me dropped to the ground.

Fear, determination, and rage battled inside me. If the dark magic inside me came from Tzanagoth, and Sterling had summoned and controlled the snake monsters. I could too.

But the moment I thought that, the dark magic stuttered, weakening and slipping out of my grasp.

It was just like the last time I'd lost control of the grimalkins, but this time I could feel it being pulled away from me from within me.

Sterling.

It had to be Sterling. We were tethered together and Whil had said that tether was the source of my dark magic.

I didn't know how or why he was involved with the merchants, maybe he'd noticed the battle and was just seizing the opportunity to hurt me, but I knew without a doubt he was responsible for the snake monsters. Even if we killed all of the grimalkins, he'd just keep sending more snakes after us until everyone I cared about was dead.

He had to be stopped, and the wildness roaring inside me along with my burning rage said I was the one who had to do it.

AUDREY

"It's Sterling," I yelled at Bishop as he tore a snake monster in two with his claws. "He's controlling the snakes. We have to stop him."

Without waiting for an answer, I took off, dashing through an opening between two wolves who were each fighting a grimalkin, and past the crumbling building where the swordsmen had made their camp.

With a growl, I concentrated on whatever was pulling on the magic inside me, determined to find its source. It had to be Sterling. How dare he try to fuck with my new life? I was finally happy and content, and that asshole had to keep coming after me.

My footsteps pounded on the uneven ground as I dodge chunks of collapsed buildings, tree roots, and broken flagstones.

Inside me, my dark magic stuttered, strong one

minute, weaker the next, and always being dragged from somewhere ahead of me.

Except was I being stupid? What made me think I could possibly stand against Sterling even with my newfound alpha power. He'd become that monster and had to be stronger and—

A new horrible realization hit me. If my alpha power did come from the dark magic and Sterling had control over it, did that mean *he* could control my alpha power?

Fuck. This was the worst idea I'd ever come up with. Sterling was going to murder me.

But my wildness howled, burning with that strange fury that threatened to consume me.

He wouldn't kill me because I wasn't a weakling anymore. *I* would kill him and my fury didn't care that I was eager to commit murder. Sterling had summoned a monster knowing it was going to eat me alive, and if my dream had been true, he'd slaughtered Mila and Porter as well.

He had to be stopped. Permanently.

And I was going to do it.

I rounded a corner and staggered to a stop. Before me lay the grand courtyard in front of Tzanagoth's towering temple. Dead center, beside the fountain with the horrifying statue of Tzanagoth eating people, stood Sterling.

He was a terrifying, living replica of the statue, twice his usual height with bright red skin, large leathery wings, and ram's horns twisting from his forehead. The only reason I recognized him was because he wore the same cruel look in his eyes and the sneer he'd always worn.

Beside him, also smirking, was Royce, except compared to Sterling he looked small and weak. I couldn't believe I'd thought he was powerful. He hadn't tortured me like Sterling had, but Royce's betrayal had been so much worse than anything Sterling had done.

He'd made me believe we were fated mates, that he'd love me for who I was and would rescue me from the nightmare I'd been living in since I was a kid.

He'd crushed the sliver of hope I'd been clinging to, cementing the idea that no one could ever want me.

Behind them, by two of the four pillars marking a large square in the middle of the courtyard, stood the tall shimmering rip between realms.

I hadn't wanted to accept it had actually returned, even though I knew Knox wouldn't lie to me and Sterling and Royce standing in front of me was undeniable proof. It being there meant my nightmare had been real.

And there, on the ground in front of the rip, lay two mangled bodies. From where I stood, it was impossible to tell who Sterling's victims were, but I knew it was Mila and Porter.

Mila had been my only friend in my old pack, the only one willing to risk Sterling's anger, and he'd brutally murdered her.

The wildness and anger within me flared, burning inside me.

"You know who that is, don't you?" Sterling asked

with a dark chuckle. "It's the stupid little girl you thought you could be friends with. Turns out with this power—" he flexed his hand and a ball of smoke whirled around his fingers, reveling in his new strength. "I don't need an incomplete mating bond. A complete one will do."

Royce joined his laughter, and my insides churned with disgust, while fear and adrenaline and dark magic pounded through me.

"If you're so powerful, why are you here?" I demanded. "You got your power. You could have stayed in our realm and led all the packs."

He wouldn't have been able to do much more than that though. There were a lot more supernatural beings in my old realm than there were here and some of them were really powerful.

Aaaaand, I'd just answered my question.

I didn't know how he'd guessed that the supers here weren't nearly as powerful as those in my realm, but he must have figured it out or decided it was worth the risk. There, he could only go so far. Here, he could rule the world.

"I'm a god, and this realm is mine." Sterling threw his head back and released a bellowing laugh, the sound cruel and dark, making my skin crawl. "*You're* mine. *My* sacrifice and I'm here to finish the job."

Sterling stretched his arms and wings out and a tidal wave of skin-crawling alpha power, just like the power I felt from the grimalkins, slammed into me.

It stole my breath and wrenched me down to my

knees, forcing me to submit to Sterling like I'd always done.

No. Get up. Get up, now.

But I couldn't make myself move. His power crushed me, stronger than anything I'd ever felt before, because I was weak and pathetic and helpless. I wasn't important. No one wanted me. Being with Bishop and Knox was a foolish fantasy because no one wanted to spend the rest of their life tied to a powerless shifter who couldn't shift.

"No!" I screamed, mentally shoving at the thoughts racing through my head, thoughts that weren't mine. They couldn't be mine.

Bishop and Knox loved me.

I. Could. Feel. It.

Our bonds assured me their love was real, and I was *not* going to give in to this asshole and let him destroy everything I'd worked for since I'd gotten here.

I heaved against his alpha power and strained to connect with my wildness and dark magic, but they, too, were crushed under Sterling's power.

"You can't do it," Sterling laughed. "I'm going to slaughter everyone you love, those new alphas of yours, and their whole pack. I'll feed on your despair."

AUDREY

"No!" I yelled back at Sterling. "I won't let you."

I had to protect my mates.

As if thinking of them summoned them, Bishop, Knox, and Cyrus rushed into the Great Square, their expressions fierce.

Knox, in his wolf form, looked practically feral, snarling with his lips curled back showing his teeth. But I couldn't sense his emotions, couldn't tell if he held onto any scrap of humanity.

I couldn't feel Bishop's emotions, either. The power crushing me and raging inside me overwhelmed everything. My stomach ached, but my rage burned through my nausea.

"Get away from her," Bishop commanded, his own alpha power crashing into the courtyard as he raced toward Sterling.

"Don't—" I gasped.

They didn't understand how powerful Sterling was. He was going to murder them.

Before they'd even gotten close to him, he flicked his hand and three men? Beings? Creatures? rose from the ground, black smoke swirling around them. They were identical, each wearing heavy clothes that hid their form and hoods that hid their faces, and they all looked like the man who'd poisoned Bishop.

"Don't let their claws touch you," Bishop yelled as the men screeched an inhuman sound and leaped toward my guys.

"It was you?" I snarled at Sterling.

My guys twisted and leaped out of the way of the smoke men's claws trying to get in a strike while I heaved and snarled. My mates needed me and I was stuck bowing on the ground. I was stronger than this.

Sterling howled with laughter. "That's it, fight me. Squirm against my power. Entertain me."

Like I'd *entertained* him when he and his friends bullied me at school and taunted me about the mother I'd never known and the father who couldn't handle living with the things he'd done in the war?

No.

No more.

My wildness surged. I seized it, wrapped it around the dark magic, and heaved. Power, stronger, wild power, roared through my veins. It tore through Sterling's demand to submit and filled me with strength as I stood.

"I'm not your toy anymore."

Sterling's sneer twisted into a snarl, rage filling his eyes. "You'll always be mine."

He raised his arms, and a flurry of snake monsters burst from the ground around me, snapping and hissing.

One of the snake monsters swooped at my head. I raised my hands to bat it away, but another dove in and wrapped around my neck, squeezing tight. Others sank their fangs into my flesh, but I couldn't feel the pain of their bites.

The dark magic pulsed, stronger and stronger, consuming me.

I had to save my men, had to stop the smoke assassins before they could be poisoned.

With a snarl, I tore the snake from around my neck and the dark magic snapped, a quick, sharp blast.

All the snakes around me burst into smoke and the smoke men screeched, crumbling to ash at my guys' feet.

Surprise and fury flashed across Sterling's expression and it was my turn to look smug.

He was going to pay for everything he'd done to me.

I glanced at my guys, but I couldn't tell if they'd been poisoned or not. But there wasn't anything I could do about it right now. Sterling had to be stopped and then I could pray that I could remove the poison using my own dark magic.

At least, for now, they were free and could help me.

But as soon as I thought that, grimalkins and snake monsters stampeded into the courtyard and they were overwhelmed again. Some of our fighters quickly followed, but not all of them, and I couldn't help worrying that they hadn't arrived because they couldn't, not because they were still fighting monsters elsewhere.

"Kill her," Sterling roared, jerking his chin at Royce. "Get me my magic,"

Royce shifted into his wolf and barreled toward me. I raised my spear, swinging it at him, but he slipped past the weapon and slammed into me, knocking me to the ground.

With a snarl, he dove in to bite me, and I swept my spear up, bashing him in the face with the shaft. He staggered to the side, and I scrambled back, desperate to get on my feet and put space between us.

I don't think so, bitch, he snarled as he lurched forward and snagged my pantleg with his teeth, jerking me closer.

Sterling howled with laughter, and my dark magic heaved within my control, while the grimalkin's alpha power grated against my skin.

I kicked at Royce's head, missed, and kicked again, my heel skimming the side of his face.

"Just fucking die," Sterling roared.

How dare he! How dare he fuck with my life.

"No. Way. In. Hell," I roared back.

I seized my alpha power and slammed it as hard as I could at Royce. I was sure I could resist Royce's command, but I had no idea if I was powerful enough to command him. He was almost as powerful as Sterling, and I had no idea if Sterling had given Royce any special power. There was just too much power and energy snapping through the air to tell.

Royce jerked to a stop and shifted back to a human, his eyes wide with shock.

"You—" he gasped.

"Me," I snarled back, satisfaction pouring through me.

Take that, asshole. I'm not weak anymore.

"Fucking useless," Sterling screamed as he stormed toward me.

Then, between one quick step and another, he shifted into... a monster.

It was more like a grimalkin than a wolf, except it was three times the size and instead of a grimalkin's short, black fur, it had red, leathery skin and a thin tail with a wicked point on the end. Large black wings rose above its body — like the gryphons' wings — and Tzanagoth's trademark ram's horns curled from its forehead.

It— Sterling pounced on Royce, still struggling against my alpha power, and chomped him in half.

My thoughts lurched, unable to fully register what had happened, and bile burned my throat.

Bones crunched, frothy pink drool dripped from Sterling's mouth, and part of Royce's arm dropped to the ground... right beside the rest of him. Legs. Half torso. All slumped on the ground surrounded by a massive pool of blood.

Horror roiled in my stomach and I stumbled back a step, drawing Sterling's attention.

Oh, fuck.

He lunged at me, black smoke and dripping blood pouring from a mouth with too many teeth. In my weak, human form, I didn't stand a chance against him.

I wrenched my spear up to strike him, but he batted it out of my hands, sending it clattering across the flagstones out of reach, then he snapped at me.

With a yelp, I dove out of the way. His teeth tore through the back of my shirt as I scrambled to direct my magic into controlling a grimalkin or snake monster to help me — since I no longer had a weapon and the monsters had overrun even my guys and no one was going to come save me.

Sterling swiped at me with his paw. I tried to leap out of the way, but he still caught me, sending me tumbling across the courtyard just like my spear.

Fuck me.

That strike could have killed me, but he'd pulled his claws. He wanted to torture me first.

I shot my dark magic toward the closest grimalkin but felt Sterling yank it away.

No. Please, no.

The magic was my only chance of surviving.

AUDREY

I PUSHED HARDER WITH MY DARK MAGIC, STRAINING TO reach the grimalkins, but the power vanished again and Sterling roared with laughter.

Pathetic, he chuckled. *Just give up and die.*

"No," I spat at him.

I'd never just give up. I hadn't through all the years he and his father had tortured me, and I wouldn't do it now. It didn't matter if all my power was from the dark magic, I'd—

My thoughts stuttered. If the dark magic had given me alpha powers, maybe it could awaken my wolf — if only for the fight.

With a new determination roaring through me, I twisted the dark magic inside me, wrapping it up with my wildness. Pain burned through my stomach and across my chest, and smoke poured from my mouth.

Sterling lunged at me, and I scrambled out of the way,

my stomach heaving, threatening to expel what little was in it at the sudden movement.

Die, Sterling roared, swiping again. *Just die and give me my power.*

I dove to the side as something snapped inside me. Agonizing pain ripped through every muscle in my body, and I screamed, collapsing to my hands and knees.

Except instead of landing on my hands and knees, I landed on white paws.

Paws.

I had paws.

Wildness coursed through my veins, singing a ferocious song of primal power, as if my soul really was fully connected, my wolf half no longer blocked by a curse cast generations ago.

But I knew it wasn't going to last. I only had my wolf because of the dark magic and as soon as Whil could figure out how to get rid of it, I'd lose my wolf — because she'd either get rid of the magic, or I'd make her lock me away before I turned into a monster like Sterling.

And none of that mattered. Sterling had to be stopped.

I wrenched my attention away from my paws to Sterling, whose eyes were blazing with fury.

Submit! Sterling roared, and a wave of power crashed toward me, aimed at crushing my will and forcing me to obey.

But my wildness flared stronger and my wolf pressed against my senses.

She'd never submit.

Never again.

She released her own wave of alpha power, shattering Sterling's wave before it could even reach me, and Sterling's eyes widened in surprise.

Yeah, my alpha power is stronger than yours, asshole. Barely, and I had no idea if I'd win the next contest of wills. Which meant I needed to end this.

Because I could. I had it in me... and if I couldn't, everyone I loved would die.

I lunged at him, snapping at his throat, but he leaped out of the way just in time. With a growl, he slashed at me with his claws. I twisted to the side, determined to dodge and attack at the same time.

But I wasn't fast enough. Sterling's claws skimmed my side, leaving behind a burning line of pain even as I managed to sink my teeth into his hind leg.

He roared, wrenching his head to snap at me, but I scrambled back before he could bite me.

We fought, him swiping and biting, his body more powerful than mine, and me dodging and nicking him, with my faster, more agile wolf.

I panted hard, and my pulse pounded as I dodged his claws again.

God damn it. No matter how hard I tried, I couldn't quite reach his throat or underbelly. There was no way I could strike a killing blow, and without a doubt, I was going to get tired before he did.

Sterling's strikes grew harder, more vicious, swatting

me this way and that, drawing more stinging lines through my skin. He roared, his movement growing jerky, and I could practically feel frustration radiating from him.

He thought I'd be easy to kill, and I'd proven him wrong.

Well, go me.

With a roar, he shifted back into his monstrous form, towering over me. His claws flew toward me, faster than the swipes he'd been taking in his wolflike form.

Oh, fuck.

I heaved myself to the left, but as I moved, a sharp yank inside my head made me stumble. Inside me, the dark magic twisted tight, no longer within my control.

Icy fear exploded in my veins, and the magic roared stronger, threatening to completely seize my muscles and render me helpless against Sterling's next strike.

He was taking my dark magic and using it against me.

No. I wrenched at my magic, desperate to regain control, while the edge of Sterling's claws tore through my side and sent me flying back.

I hit the ground with a heavy thump that knocked the breath from my lungs, agony screaming through me.

Sharp pain snapped through my head and I fought to stand.

Get up. Just get up.

I had to fight him, but he was in my head. His alpha power hadn't worked on me, so he was using the tether binding us together to manipulate me... just like he'd manipulated me in my dreams to hurt myself.

I gritted my teeth, desperate to keep him out and hold onto my magic, but his power ripped into every cell, and suddenly my paws were hands.

I screamed, my body trembling, getting weaker and weaker, melting back into the nothing I was before I'd met my guys. The rage that had been burning through me flickered, melting into a pinprick of anger, and my soul wept and my wolf howled.

"That's it. Despair. Know that when you're dead, I'm going to tear your alphas limb from limb."

"I won't let you," I gasped back.

"You can't stop me. You're nothing without my power," he sneered, his enormous frame towering over me while I panted, naked on my hands and knees. "You'll always be nothing. You're only good for a sacrifice. Now finish your fate and die."

He lunged at me, his claws already dripping with my blood, and I threw myself back, narrowly escaping his attack.

I crashed onto the flagstones, my arms flung wide but they did little to soften the fall. The impact rattled up my butt and back until my head slammed against the ground. Sparks of black and brilliant light flashed across my vision and my breath burst from my lungs with a whoosh.

I gasped, fighting to breathe as Sterling swiped again.

My pulse roared, my mind screaming at me to move, get up, do something!

I heaved to the side, the world lurching out of focus, and my hand hit my spear.

My ferocious wildness surged, and I thrust my spear up, shoving the tip with all my strength, determination and desperation into Sterling's heart.

The force of his forward movement to reach me pushed the spear deeper into his body, and his eyes widened in shock.

Mine widened in shock as well.

I'd killed him.

A shifter couldn't heal a massive hole in his heart fast enough to save him.

I shoved him to the side so he didn't collapse on top of me and wrenched out the spear. His blood poured onto the flagstones, pooling around my bare feet, but I couldn't stop staring at him.

The monster who'd tormented me from the moment I'd been forced to move into his home with him and his father, who'd tricked me into thinking I'd found my fated mate and had tried to sacrifice me to a monster that was going to eat me alive, was dead.

He couldn't control me anymore, couldn't manipulate me through my dreams, and would never hurt anyone else.

I was finally free.

AUDREY

RELIEF RUSHED THROUGH ME AS I SAGGED BACK AGAINST the flagstones and swept my gaze over the courtyard. With Sterling dead, the snake monsters burst into smoke and vanished and the grimalkins paused mid-fight and shook their heads. Cyrus took advantage of the distraction and killed the grimalkin in front of him, spurring on the others who made short work of the remaining beasts.

Thank, God. It was over.

The medics that had been standing at the edge of the battle, rushed to treat the injured, one heading toward Bishop, who waved him away before taking off his clothes and shifting into his wolf.

Healing his injuries while shifting would drain him, but it meant he wasn't tying up a medic. Knox, who'd fought as a wolf, shifted to his human form to heal and together they walked toward me.

I could feel their love and worry for me rushing

through our mating bonds, and my heart swelled with joy. Mine. They were mine.

With that thought, I reached out with the dark magic, searching for signs of the horrible poison. All three of my guys had been poisoned, but before I could freeze in fear, the magic dove into their bodies and, drawing a scream from all three of them, ripped the poison out.

They were safe and it was over.

Finally.

Except the dark magic inside me didn't settle after removing the poison, it grew stronger and stronger, whirling in and around me, stealing my breath.

My stomach cramped and I dropped to my knees. Bile burned up my throat and across my tongue, and I heaved forward, black smoke pouring out of my mouth.

Panic raced through my mating bonds, but I could barely sense it with the dark magic roaring through me.

"Get a medic!" Knox yelled.

He raced to my side, dropped to his knees, and pulled me into his arms. Desperation filled his wolf-darkened gaze, and his alpha power stuttered against my power as he fought to stay in control and not go feral.

Audrey, Bishop said in my head as he pressed his wet nose against my bare thigh.

I could tell he wanted to hold me as well, needed the physical contact to calm his wolf, but knew he couldn't crowd me. The medic needed space to help me and Bishop couldn't take me away from Knox who'd completely lose it if he wasn't holding me.

A second later, Cyrus skidded to a stop beside us, his eyes so dark I wasn't sure who was in control of his body, the human or the wolf. He brushed my hair away from my face as he made space for a medic who thankfully knew enough to not take me from Knox.

I gasped for air, the dark magic growing stronger and stronger and a heavy exhaustion dragging on my limbs. My back heaved, and I vomited up more smoke and bile half onto the ground and half into Cyrus's lap.

"It's going to be okay," he said, not caring about the mess.

"She's bumped her head and has a whole bunch of lacerations that need bandaging," the medic said. "But that doesn't explain the smoke."

"Something has to explain it," Knox snarled.

"It's the darkness inside her," Whil said, nudging the medic out of the way and placing a hand on my forehead, as the medic started binding my wounds. "This close to Tzanagoth's resting place, I can tell the dark magic is his, and it's rushing into her."

"How is it rushing into her?" Cyrus demanded.

"The tether is also gone," Whil replied. "We suspected it was connected to Sterling and now that he's dead all of Tzanagoth's power is pouring into Audrey."

My stomach cramped and I bit back a moan. The guys flickered in and out of focus, and I struggled to keep my eyes open.

If she's getting all of Tzanagoth's power... Bishop said.

"Then the curse on the realm is putting her to sleep," Whil finished.

"You don't know that," Knox snarled.

"She's already on the verge of passing out," Cyrus snapped back then turned to Whil. "Do something. Save her."

"I can't. I'm not strong enough and there isn't anyone in our realm who is," Whil replied.

I raised a trembling hand to caress Knox's cheek but couldn't lift it high enough before the exhaustion dragged it back down. "It'll be okay."

"Nothing will be okay." His voice cracked and my heart broke for him.

He hadn't wanted a mate in the first place and I'd accidentally bound myself to him— No, *fate* had bound us together. It hadn't been an accident at all. Except now I could feel in my soul that living without me, even if I was in a coma, would shatter him.

His grip around me tightened. "I can't lose you."

Bishop whimpered and Cyrus raked his hands through his hair.

"If you can get to Faerie, you can find a sorcerer strong enough to save you," Whil told me. "But that means I have to open a rip."

My gaze slowly dragged up past Cyrus's shoulder to the far side of the courtyard, searching for the rip. Last I'd seen it, it was too thin for us to go through without us touching the sides and turning to ash. Whil would need to use her magic to widen it, but surely that was easier than creating a new one. But even as I searched for it, I knew the telltale shimmer was gone. It had died with Sterling.

Do you have enough power to open a rip? Bishop asked. *I'm sure you thought about it in the past and you're still trapped in this realm.*

Sadness filled Whil's expression. "I've figured out how Sterling opened the first rip, but—"

But she needed an incomplete mating bond to do it. That was the toll Sterling had made me pay the first time and it had to be the toll now. Except I'd never ask someone to bond with me or anyone else just to create a rip between realms.

"I'll do it," Cyrus said. "I'll bond with Audrey."

My soul soared at his words even as my heart plummeted. He was my mate. We were meant to be together, but I couldn't let him bond with me, no matter how much I wanted it.

And I sure as hell didn't want him mate bonding with me because he felt it was his duty. I wanted him to love me like I loved him.

"No," I said, trying to sound firm and failing, my voice coming out breathy and weak. "If Whil can't make a rip and I fall asleep, you won't be able to seal the bond. You'll go crazy."

"I don't care about that," he said.

"And if she can open a rip and we can't get back?" I asked. "What then?"

"You're not going through the rip without me," he snarled.

"You can't, the pack needs you." Why was he being so insistent? He couldn't just abandon his pack.

"But I need *you*." He cupped my cheeks with his palms, forcing me to look at him. "I've given up a lot of things for my pack, put myself last my entire life, but I won't give up you. I can't."

The heat from his touch seared through my skin, raced down my neck, and swelled around my heart.

Mine. He was mine.

The warmth of our shifter connection was as strong as my connection with Bishop and Knox.

"I love you," he said. "I've loved you from the first moment you woke in the Residence terrified of me, a spark of defiance in your eyes." He squeezed his eyes shut, and a single tear released and trailed down his cheek. "You're my mate, Audrey. You've always been."

My heart sang as my soul wept.

It was too late... but it was better this way.

If he didn't bond with me, he was safe. He wouldn't die from a broken heart or go crazy. There was no guarantee that Whil could make the rip or that we'd be able to find a fae sorcerer who could help us.

Cyrus turned to Whil. "I'm bonding with Audrey and you're making a rip." His attention jumped back to me. "I can't live without you. Please. Let me do this for you. Take me as your mate."

My throat tightened. It was clear in his eyes that he

wouldn't take no for an answer and I didn't want to tell him no. I wanted to say yes, wanted to yell it so everyone could hear that my soul was finally fully complete. Cyrus was mine. It was fate and I didn't want to run away from it.

"Yes," I told him, my voice barely a whisper. "I accept your bond."

Joy filled his expression, and he brushed his lips against mine in a soft, quick, heartbreaking kiss.

"It could be a one-way trip," Whil warned. "I've done the research and there's something about the gods' power that's unique to them that the curse gloms onto. The gates to this realm are safe to open, but if the Fae elders refuse to unlock them or you can't find someone who can create another rip, you won't be able to return."

So be it, Bishop said.

"*We* won't return—?" I asked. Whil wasn't including herself. "Whil, this is a chance to go to Faerie. You can finally go home."

Whil's expression softened and she took my hand. "I know. For a long time, I wanted to go back, wanted to talk to and be with other fae, but I can't leave Stonehaven. This pack is my family. There are so many people here I love and care for. In Faerie, I'm barely a sorcerer, but here, my sorcerer ability doesn't matter."

I weakly squeezed her hand, understanding how she felt. I needed to be helpful, too. I hadn't realized how much I wanted a pack until I'd stumbled into this realm.

Now that I had one with people who I knew in my soul I needed to protect, I didn't want to leave.

But I also didn't want to fall asleep and never wake up, and I didn't know how me being in a coma would affect Bishop and Knox. Would they be fine or would they slowly start to go crazy as if their mating bonds were dying?

KNOX

I CLUTCHED AUDREY AGAINST MY CHEST, MY WOLF HOWLING and raging inside me.

I hadn't wanted to be mated to anyone, hadn't thought with my issues that I deserved a mate, and I'd tried so hard to force her away.

I'd told myself we had to break our bond because I couldn't give her the kind of life she deserved. I couldn't stand large crowds or be indoors for more than a handful of hours depending on the size of the space, and it would be cruel to force her to spend the rest of her life with that.

Having a mate meant change and I'd been barely holding onto my humanity as it was.

But in truth, I was afraid. If I opened up to her, she'd know just how afraid I was. She'd see the scared pup who'd been trapped in that cave-in, pinned under all that rock for days. She'd see the beast I'd let myself become to protect that pup.

"Knox," she whispered, her breath warm against my skin.

"I've got you," I said, trying to not let my panic color my tone or bleed through our mating bond. She had to be scared enough by being filled with all that evil magic. I couldn't add the feralness screaming through my soul threatening to completely take over. *I love you.*

Sisters, I loved her so much.

Audrey had become an irreplaceable part of my life. I hadn't told her the truth about my claustrophobia but I had no doubt that she saw the real me. And still, she embraced our accidental mating bond, loving me softly, deeply, and wholeheartedly.

Before her, I'd preferred the wild isolation of my wolf. I'd even let my humanity slip to the background and let my wolf take over. But now, with her by my side, I found myself more comfortable in my human skin, able to spend more time around people and indoors. It was a change I never expected, but one I welcomed for her sake.

Because I *wanted* to do all those things I couldn't do for her. I *wanted* to spend the night, every night, indoors in her bed loving her, wanted to meet with her friends and be social. I wanted to give her the world.

The feralness heaved and my wolf snarled.

I had to protect her, save her. Something. Gods damned something. Now.

"Knox, please," she murmured, her voice barely audible.

"Stay awake, Audrey," my wolf growled, my grip on her tightening. "Stay awake."

Stay with me.

I needed to say more, engage her in conversation to keep her from falling asleep while Bishop, Cyrus, and Whil figured out how to save her. But all I could think of was holding her tight and screaming.

Mine. She was mine. I refused to let her go. If she slept forever, so would I. My wolf and I both agreed.

The feralness could have us. We'd let it consume our consciousness and become the beast everyone thought we were. We were nothing without Audrey.

We didn't want to be anything without her.

Audrey moaned, reminding me that we hadn't lost her yet. She was fighting the gods' curse and we needed to fight for her too.

"I saw your wolf," I blurted out, saying the first thing that came to mind, determined to keep her awake.

Her eyelids drooped, and I gave her a little shake, waking her up.

"Your wolf," I said. "She's beautiful. You have to see her. All white and small. Fast as lightning. We're going to run together through the pack's primary grove once this is over."

My throat tightened as she fought to open her eyes.

"Promise me we'll run together," I insisted, my voice breaking. "Audrey, promise me."

I gave her another soft shake and she groaned, dragging her gaze back to me.

I promise, she said in my head, her telepathy awakening with her wolf.

Love and sadness poured through our mating bond and I pressed my lips to her forehead.

Please, don't leave me.

"Knox." Cyrus's voice jerked me out of my thoughts, reminding me that I was a ferocious beast who'd do anything to protect his mate.

Why the fuck was I sitting there panicking and wallowing?

Because *I* couldn't save her. We were already mate bonded, so I couldn't make an incomplete bond with her, and I wasn't a sorcerer and couldn't just rip the magic out of her.

I couldn't do anything except cling to her like my life depended on it... because it did. Life wouldn't be worth living without her.

"We can't stay in Anakar," Cyrus said, his brow furrowed with concern. "Tzanagoth's spirits could still come out once night falls, and I don't want to risk them screwing everything up."

"Then let's go," I said as I stood.

With Tzanagoth's power rushing into Audrey, I didn't know if his spirits still existed, or if they'd follow us when we left, but it was still smart to leave.

Bishop nodded his agreement, and the four of us marched to where the rest of our party had gathered.

"Deacon," Cyrus said, capturing our betas attention.

"You'll need to take charge of the pack while we save Audrey."

The big man nodded, his alpha power stuttered over us like it always did. "You got it."

"We may not return," Cyrus said, his tone thick with emotion. "This could be a one-way trip for the four of us."

Deacon grabbed his shoulder and gave him a fierce grin. "If I found my mate, I'd do whatever it took, too."

"Get our men out of Anakar by nightfall," Cyrus commanded then he called for Folmar to help us return to Stonehaven.

Without question, Folmar called over two other gryphon shifters, and they all shifted and knelt so we could climb onto their backs. With a screech, they took off into the air, racing back to Stonehaven.

It was my first time flying — and from the way my stomach lurched my last — but I couldn't even try to enjoy the trip. My focus remained solely on my mate who was completely limp in my arms, her breathing slow and steady.

The landscape below blurred together, and it felt like an eternity before we finally arrived at the sacred grove on the Residence's property even though it had probably only been a few hours.

Nova and Finn waited for us. Once we'd gotten close enough to town, Cyrus must have told Nova what we needed. They greeted us with fresh clothes and wet towels, so we could clean up after our fight. They'd also packed three packs that included a few healing elixirs, changes of clothes, rations, and a purse with some small gems in case we needed to pay the fae sorcerer to save Audrey.

Carefully holding Audrey, I climbed off Folmar, thanking her gruffly and joining the others. Audrey needed to get cleaned up and changed, she'd be mortified if we took her anywhere unconscious and naked, but I couldn't make myself let her go.

"Here," Nova said gently, handing me a cloth before dribbling two healing elixirs into Audrey's mouth.

"Thanks," I murmured, my attention devoted to Audrey as I wiped away the traces of blood and dirt from her fragile body.

Her eyelids fluttered, making my heart leap, and I gave her a gentle shake, waking her up.

That's it, beautiful, Bishop said. *Stay with us. Just for a little longer. Cyrus needs to profess his love to you for this to work.*

She groaned and, with great effort, opened her eyes wide.

"When you get through the rip, you'll need to find a powerful fae sorcerer capable of extracting the dark magic," Whil instructed. "I can only create a rip to Audrey's realm because our realms are so closely linked, and I can't open a gate directly to Faerie, so you're going to have to find someone who can get you there."

"If you can—" Audrey sucked in a deep breath, struggling to stay awake, while Nova bound her wounds and helped me slide on Audrey's dress — which was easier than trying to dress her in a shirt and pants. "Find a JP agent. They're watchmen for supers in my realm. If they can't get us through a gate to Faerie, they'll know someone who can."

We'll find one, Bishop promised, and I could feel a determination coming through our twin bond that matched mine. *Cyrus, let's do this.*

Cyrus moved to kneel before Audrey, still clutched in my protective embrace. He raised both hands and cradled her face, urging her to meet his gaze. His eyes were filled with sorrow and love and my wolf howled for him.

Cyrus was Audrey's mate as well and even I could tell he'd been an idiot, pushing her away to protect her then putting our pack first, trying to clear up the mess with the merchants before telling her how much he cared.

And now here he was, finally telling her the truth when we could lose her forever.

"I'm so sorry for ever making you doubt yourself and for scaring you," Cyrus said, his voice low. "I swear to spend every day showing you how much you mean to me."

Audrey raised a trembling hand and brushed his cheek, her smile soft and sad.

The vow, Bishop reminded, and Cyrus drew in a steadying breath.

"Blessed be the Great Sisters and her children, and blessed be my sacred vow," Cyrus recited, his eyes turning glassy with tears. "You're my love, my life. My soul recognizes yours as my mate, and I, without reservation, bind my soul with yours for eternity. I love you, Audrey."

"Mine," Audrey said, her words slurred, "Finally."

Whil drew close and gestured for Nova and Finn to give us our packs.

"Get ready." She raised her hands, and her soft, perpetual golden glow exploded in a brilliant light.

A sharp gust of wind swept through the grove and the ground trembled. Whil groaned and dropped to her knees, her eyes squeezed tight and her jaw clenched shut. Her breathing turned short and sharp, and her body shook.

Then, with a sharp *crack*, the air in front of us ripped open revealing a dark field and a forest in the distance. Just like the rip in Anakar, this one was tall, with shimmering edges, but thankfully it was also wide enough to go through.

I tightened my grip on Audrey and stepped up beside Cyrus with Bishop, still in his wolf form, on my other side.

We'll save you, I swore.

Even if I had to let my beast consume me to do it.

BISHOP

Fear tightened my chest. The thought of seeing Audrey unconscious every day and not being able to talk to her or share my life with her making it hard to breathe. She wouldn't be dead. But she wouldn't be alive, either, and I couldn't live with that.

She was too amazing to lose, sweet and shy and funny, with a heart filled with so much love. She was fierce, too. She didn't show it often, but she did when it mattered, and Sisters, she'd shown her ferocious warrior spirit when she'd faced Sterling.

That monster had actually been a monster. He'd looked like the horrible god depicted in the statue outside of Tzanagoth's temple, and she hadn't flinched or hid or even looked afraid. She'd been a goddess of vengeance and justice, and Sterling had deserved everything that had come to him.

And straight ahead lay her salvation.

I stared at the rip between the realms alongside Cyrus and Knox. Whil had used Cyrus's incomplete mating bond with Audrey to create the rip, and while it was the only way to get to a fae sorcerer who might be able to help, I feared for my brother.

We had no idea how long it would take us to get to Faerie and find a sorcerer, and he'd been fighting with his attraction to Audrey before he'd permanently bound his soul to hers. Sure, it was supposed to take a while before the urge from the bond to seal it became overwhelming, but given how much I knew he already loved her, I was certain we didn't have a while.

I chuffed and raised my snout to Knox, who held Audrey, then to Cyrus who stood beside him. Whil had cast the spell, there was no going back, and none of us would go back if we could. All that mattered was saving our mate.

Together we stepped through the rip, careful not to touch the shimmering edges. A shiver rolled through my body, the only indication that we were passing between realms, and then we were in Audrey's realm.

A warm summer night engulfed us, a cool contrast to the mid-day sun that we'd just left. We stood in a field of low grass and right in the middle of a fight... or rather a massacre.

Four men surrounded a man and a woman with strangely mottled skin. Their clothes were ripped and deep gouges — the kind made from small claws — scored their torsos. They lay limp half on the ground and half in the men's arms, all of the men pressed close, one with his lips against the woman's neck in an open-mouthed kiss, another at the man's throat, and the two others lapping at the gashes across their torsos.

What the fuck?

We hadn't been able to see them because of the limited view through the rip even though they were only a few feet away, and every instinct I had screamed that we had to get out of here.

One of the men jerked his head and hissed at us, revealing sharp fangs and blood dribbling down his chin.

My pulse lurched. Audrey had said all manner of supernatural beings — supers as she called them — lived in her realm, and now I was standing face to face with a mythological vampire.

One that looked hungry as hell and, if the stories I'd read were correct, was going to be hard to stop. According to the lore, vampires could move faster than a shifter and could heal at a phenomenal rate.

The other vampires looked up and hissed, their eyes black, their expressions hungry and smug.

"Shit," Knox growled, tensing beside me while a wild rage blasted through our twin bond.

"What do we have here?" a big, bulky vampire asked.

"I think they brought us dessert," another one hissed. This guy was small for a man, but I didn't doubt he was any less dangerous.

"I think both of us should pretend we didn't see anything," Cyrus snarled, his hands flexing and his claws extending from his fingertips. "You don't want this to turn into a fight."

"The puppy thinks he can fight us?" a heavyset vampire laughed and the boringly average looking vampire beside him joined in.

"This puppy knows he can." Cyrus's alpha power rolled off of him revealing just how determined he was.

He knew his power wouldn't affect the vampires, but I doubted he could help himself. Knox was radiating almost as much alpha power as Cyrus, and I could feel mine pouring off me in waves as well.

We'd do anything to protect our mate, and while Cyrus had done a shit job at diffusing the situation, we all knew nothing we said was going to change the vampire's minds.

They can move fast, I said in Cyrus's and Knox's head, the warning only a second before the vampires shot toward us.

Cyrus lunged forward to meet the attack, while Knox jerked out of reach of the heavyset vampire, protecting Audrey with his body and leaving his side open to the vampire's claws.

I bunched down, ready to leap at the heavyset man as his claws dragged through Knox's side, but before I could move, Knox shoved Audrey at me. Darkness filled his eyes and feralness radiated through our bond as he shifted into his wolf form. His wolf had taken over and had already figured out I was the weakest link in this fight.

I'd taken a serious swipe from a grimalkin's claws and had to shift out my injuries, but that had tired me out. I was sure Knox was also tired, but he was a natural born hunter and the feral side of his wolf would keep him going longer than me.

With a huff, I shifted, grabbing Audrey before she fell on the ground. Exhaustion crashed through me, but I forced myself to my feet, determined to put space between me and the fight.

The small vampire rushed toward me, but Cyrus shoved the average looking vampire into the small one making them stumble away from me.

"Get her out of here," Cyrus barked at me, his power snapping into my soul but not forcing me to obey.

Beside him, Knox bit a chunk out of the heavyset vampire's leg, making the vampire howl with pain. The guy staggered but righted himself and dove for Knox.

Again, I turned to run, but the large vampire blocked me.

Fucking hell.

He dove at me, his movements so fast I could barely follow them. Somehow, I manage to jerk out of the way, protecting Audrey from his claws.

But I wasn't fast enough to save myself. Fiery pain sliced through my shoulder and the vampire sneered at me while licking his fingertips.

"You taste good, puppy." His smile grew smug.

And you taste disgusting, Knox mentally yelled at him,

making him turn toward Knox just as Knox leaped at him.

Knox's wolf, like mine and Cyrus's, was massive, and he easily tackled the vampire to the ground. With a snarl, he latched his teeth into the vampire's throat and ripped through his flesh.

One of the other vampires screamed, and I glanced up to see Cyrus tearing his claws through the average looking vampire's stomach. The man dropped to his knees, clutching at his insides and Cyrus rammed his knee into the guy's head.

The other two vampires also lay on the ground. The small guy was completely unconscious, his torso shredded by wolf claws, while the heavyset vampire rolled on the ground, moaning, both of his legs gnawed down to the bone and a deep set of claw marks tearing down his side.

Mine, Knox roared as he tipped his head back and howled. Feralness crackled through his alpha power and he stalked toward the heavyset vampire.

"Don't," Cyrus commanded, knowing that Knox was going to finish the man off. "We need to get out of here. We can't get caught with these bodies. We have to find a way to Faerie."

Knox snapped at him and Cyrus's power crushed around us.

"Audrey doesn't need us in prison or spending hours being questioned by the authorities," Cyrus added.

Fine, Knox growled.

I looked up to see where we could go to clean up and for me to put on clothes, as a monster — no, a man? — swooped down from the sky on wide leathery wings.

He was enormous, broader in the chest and easily a foot taller than Cyrus. He also looked a lot like the statue of Tzanagoth back in Anakar with his wings spread out behind him and thin, tall horns protruding from his forehead.

A red mist swirled around him, setting my nerves on edge, and fury radiated off him in almost palpable waves.

Knox growled, the sound low and dangerous, and Cyrus widened his stance, ready for a fight.

Except I knew there was no way we could win a fight against him. That wasn't to say I wouldn't die protecting Audrey, or that my brothers wouldn't die to get me and Audrey a chance to escape, but the conclusion was inevitable. The man radiated power and danger and confidence.

The heavyset vampire groaned and rolled to his hands and knees as if he were going to stand, but the red mist shot out from the winged man's hand and twisted around the vampire's throat.

"If you want to live, stay down," he said, his voice low and commanding. "I don't care that the JP are on their way. I will kill you."

The JP, I mentally said to Cyrus and Knox. *Audrey said to find a JP agent.*

"So, you four," the winged man said, his narrow-eyed gaze sliding over our bodies, taking in our ragged state as well, no doubt assessing how dangerous we were.

"Wrong place, wrong time," I said with a shrug, trying to keep my voice light and praying Cyrus didn't get all possessive, aggressive wolf on him like he had with the vampires. "We'll just be on our—"

A flash of white above and behind the winged man caught my attention and my thoughts stalled.

It was another man, but instead of leathery wings his were softly glowing white feathers and pale light radiated from his eyes.

"An angel," I gasped.

Holy Sisters! I was about to meet an angel.

The angel landed beside the winged man, his gaze on the man and the woman, his expression grim.

"There has to be a way to stop this, Voth," the angel said.

"If I kill the city's new master another idiot will take his place." The winged man, Voth, shot the angel an exasperated look. "And the JP will arrest me."

"Not if that idiot walks onto your property," the angel mumbled under his breath, his words shocking me.

Everything I'd read about angels said they were upholders of law and justice, and this angel was condoning murder.

What else had I read that wasn't true?

The angel turned his attention to us. "You four should come with me."

My stomach churned at his words. I gripped Audrey

tighter and took a step back, while Cyrus tensed, and Knox growled, his hackles rising.

The angel frowned. "You're hurt. You need medical attention."

"We're fine. We've got stuff in our packs." I jerked my thumb to where we'd dropped our packs during the vampire fight. "We really should be going."

"You're not going anywhere," Voth said, his red mist billowing around him. "You're going to tell me who the fuck you are. That girl is radiating so much evil power I'm sure anyone with a hint of magical sensitivity can feel it from the next state over."

I didn't know what all that meant, but without a doubt, it was bad.

You run. I'll hold him off, Cyrus said.

No, I snapped back. He and Audrey couldn't afford to get separated.

I'll hold them, Knox snarled.

But with Knox barely clinging to himself, he wouldn't stop fighting until Voth killed him.

Fuck.

Fuck fuck fuck.

The authorities were coming, and if we refused to say something, Voth would tell them we were dangerous. That was what I'd do.

Cyrus opened his mouth to speak but without a doubt that was going to be a disaster so I inched forward.

"It's a long story," I said, trying to keep my voice steady despite my pounding heart.

I had no idea if the man-monster — that looked too much like Tzanagoth — would believe us, but I had a feeling he'd know if we were lying.

Praying that the truth would save us — and save Audrey — I sucked in a steadying breath. "Our mate is possessed by an evil power that's putting her to sleep. We've come from our realm through a rip between realms to this one to find a way into Faerie so we can find a fae sorcerer who can save her."

Voth shot the angel a strange look. It wasn't angry, but it wasn't compassionate understanding, either.

"I'll call him," the angel said as he pulled a thin rectangular box from his pocket.

"Priam," Voth warned before glaring at us. "Fae sorcerers aren't cheap. Can you pay?"

"We can," Cyrus replied as the angel, Priam, rolled his eyes and huffed. "We just need to know where to find him."

"They're mates and they've crossed realms to save her." Priam touched the surface of the rectangular box and it lit up with a bright light. "I'll tell Amiah and she'll make him do it for free."

"He's going to be pissed if you keep doing that," Voth said, but his tone had softened and the red swirling mist thinned.

Cyrus stepped forward, his alpha power still rippling around him, his body still tense. "If you just tell us where he is, we'll talk to him."

"You're not leaving here until I've healed you," Priam

said before putting the rectangle to his ear, turning his back on us, and telling someone named Bane to get to the hotel.

"You're also safest here," Voth added as red mist burst around him and his wings and horns vanished, leaving just an enormous man in strangely tailored clothes.

"I'm saying fated mates keep showing up on my doorstep and I've resigned myself to my role in all this."

My wolf whined inside me at his tone. Resigned was the right word. We weren't sure how, but we could tell he wanted more... except I wasn't sure what that meant.

"Come on," Priam said, grabbing our packs. "There's a clinic at the back of the theatre."

I shot Cyrus a wary glance and he shrugged. It didn't matter how understanding Voth seemed, it was clear he wasn't going to let us go. Audrey was too dangerous. Running wasn't an option. We had no choice but to follow the honest-to-goodness angel.

CYRUS

My body burned with need and my hard-as-hell cock ached and wept precum. It hadn't even been an hour since I'd said the vow to create a mating bond with Audrey, and already I was burning up inside to seal it.

Why had I waited so damn long to tell her how I felt?

Sisters, I was so stupid to put the pack first. Bishop had been right, it shouldn't have mattered what was going on even though I hadn't wanted to risk being killed and hurting Audrey because we'd bonded.

Inside me, my wolf paced restlessly, as desperate as I was to get the dark magic out of her and wake her up while my soul screamed at me to save her, wake her, love her.

Please. I'd do anything, risk anything, for her.

With Audrey carried protectively in Bishop's arms and Knox in his wolf form, we followed the angel, Priam, across the field with the strangely short grass toward a large, ten-story building with purple-tinted windows. The structure loomed two hundred feet away on top of a hill and was separated from us by a stretch of hard, black earth that reeked of unfamiliar smells, and held a bizarre collection of large metal and glass boxes on wheels.

I glanced over my shoulder at Voth's massive shadow still standing behind us. He'd looked more human when his wings and horns had disappeared but without a doubt he wasn't, and I knew if we tried to make a break for it, he'd hunt us down.

Of course, making a break would mean we'd be back to the drawing board looking for someone to get us into Faerie while being dangerously unfamiliar with this realm. And that wasn't good for Audrey.

At least here in Voth's custody — I wasn't going to fool myself and think the situation was anything else — a fae sorcerer was coming to us.

If he wasn't lying.

Which he could be. But all my instincts said the angel wasn't.

I hadn't read any of the books Bishop had about mythical beings from other realms I was never going to meet, so I had no idea what angel personalities were like. Priam had even suggested Voth lure someone onto his territory so Voth could kill him. But even then, the angel's frustration had been because whoever was at war with the man-monster who owned this territory was killing people. No, I believed Priam's words to be true and that he genuinely wanted to help.

And please, Sisters, help.

I turned my attention to Audrey, barely able to look away long enough to avoid walking into the metal boxes on wheels. Even in the moonlight it was clear her skin was too pale, and she hung limp in Bishop's arms, far too still even for someone fast asleep.

My throat tightened and I wanted to howl with frustration. She'd just found herself, her confidence, her power, and her wolf. This couldn't be how it ended. My mate deserved a long, amazing life, filled with Knox's passion and Bishop's laughter.

On top of that, she'd made friends in Stonehaven who I know were going to be upset if she was gone. Nova and Deacon had taken a liking to her, and Finn, much to my surprise had fully submitted to her as a pack alpha and begged her not to banish him from the pack.

And of course, she hadn't. She was grace and love and forgiveness. She was what a true alpha was supposed to be. She'd risked her life to protect her pack while also gently nurturing them.

I hadn't realized how much our pack and me and my brothers had needed her until she'd crashed into our lives and changed everything.

"This way," Priam said, his voice soft, almost soothing.

He turned away from a grand entrance fully lit by light streaming through the windows of the double doors along with bright lights attached to the brickwork. We walked around down a hill to a tucked-away side of the building, where an enormous door stood beside a smaller, human-sized one, making me even more wary.

My wolf growled low within us, suddenly concerned that he was taking us away from potential help... although really, given our reception when we'd entered this realm, I couldn't count on anyone inside helping us.

Except the angel hadn't lied.

I was sure of that.

But Sisters, it was hard to trust him when the life of my mate was on the line and when all I wanted to do was bury myself inside her and claim her.

Mine.

Always.

Priam opened the human-sized door and walked inside, and I glanced at Knox. Alpha power rolled off him in great waves and his body shook with tension. His ears flattened and he snarled, but followed the angel, and I prayed he'd be able to hold on long enough to help Audrey.

He wasn't going to leave her side until he knew she was safe, but I could tell he was barely holding on to his human consciousness. And I wasn't surprised he hadn't shifted into his human form and taken her from Bishop, even though he needed her to calm himself. His instincts were going wild, just like mine, and if he shifted, he'd exhaust himself. He couldn't protect her if he was unconscious.

Inside, the space opened up into a vast rectangular area filled with a strange, smooth, grayish-white stone. At the back sat a platform that stood at chest height for me and along the righthand wall were a set of stairs, also made from the strange stone.

We followed Priam up the stairs to a metal door, into a plan white hall with stark lights running along the ceiling, where he finally stopped about ten feet down at a small room.

Or rather, a medium-sized room that looked small because a glass wall blocked off the back third. It was crammed with two narrow beds like the bed Nova used in triage, a counter, cupboards, a sink, and a whole array of odd equipment.

"Set her on that bed and let me look at you guys," Priam said as he headed to the sink and washed his hands.

Bishop gently laid Audrey on the bed, his expression a mix of worry and determination while I sat on the other bed, fighting the urge to reach out and touch her, to feel her warmth again, to love her like she deserved.

My precum now dampened the front of my pants, and my cock throbbed as my soul screamed to complete the bond.

But I couldn't, not with her unconscious. She needed to say the vow too, or bond with me like she'd bonded with Bishop and Knox. But I couldn't feel that connection within me, only the burning need threatening to consume me.

Knox snarled, his body tense, ready to attack if Priam blinked in the wrong way.

I was sure the angel noticed — who wouldn't notice a wolf the size of a pony in the middle of their medical clinic? — but he just pulled out gauze and tape and a few other things from the cupboards, set them on a metal tray on wheels, and rolled it over to me.

"Can I touch you?" Priam asked, gesturing toward me. "I'm blessed with the ability to heal. I won't use it if you don't want—" He gestured to the tray. "But it would be faster. I can sense without touching any of you that you're exhausted, and I wouldn't recommend shifting until you've rested. Healing your injuries will help."

I gave him a tight nod and he gently set his hands against my chest. Soft white light radiated around his hands, and a warmth flooded through me that only made my longing for Audrey burn hotter.

The gashes on my arms from the vampires' claws sealed shut as I watched, and I blinked, unable to fully believe that my flesh was mending right before my eyes.

"Oh wow," Bishop breathed. "When the book said angels could heal any wound, I never imagined..."

"If you're not familiar with it, it can look unreal," Priam chuckled. "Like a movie on fast forward or something."

That had been the thing Audrey had tried to explain to Bishop when we'd headed north to break her mating bond with Knox.

My heart ached at the thought. Fuck. I needed her so much. She was mine. She'd always been mine and my wolf was furious at me for being a fucking idiot.

I was about to hop off the table and crawl onto her bed and lie beside her when two men strode into the clinic, making the small room feel even smaller.

Knox hunched, his muscles bunching ready for attack, and he growled, threatening the newcomers. They weren't enormous men like me, but they both had an aura about them that screamed power. It wasn't nearly as much as Voth, but enough that I didn't want to start a fight with them if I didn't have to.

Knox, I said, fighting to keep my mental voice calm. *They could be help.*

They better be help, he snarled back, his attention never leaving the men.

The first guy was strikingly handsome, with blue eyes so pale they were almost clear and spiky white-and-silver hair. His ears were pointed, marking him as the fae sorcerer Priam had called, although his ears were only half the size of Whil's, and his perpetual full-body fae glow — which was a soft white instead of Whil's gold— was only half as strong. A hint of black tattoos poked out from his shirtsleeves and snaked up from the collar of his dress shirt, and everything about him screamed cocky confidence with a dark edge.

The other man was so beautiful he stole my breath even as my need for Audrey erupted into a scorching volcano and made me pant. Little horns poked through his shoulder-length sandy blood hair and his presence screamed sex. Raw, unbridled, mind-blowing sex... something I needed with Audrey. Now now now.

I clench my teeth, biting back a groan, and fought to stay in control of myself. I just needed to wait a little longer. If, of course, these men were actually going to help.

Fuck, I'd make them help if they wouldn't.

It didn't matter that the odds were fifty-fifty of winning a fight against them. I would save my mate and I would claim her.

"So," the fae said, his expression dark, his attention already on Audrey. "Voth said you're from another realm."

"Don't look at her," I snarled.

His sharp gaze snapped to mine, capturing me in endless ice, before the other man bumped him with his elbow and pressed a hand over his heart.

The fae sighed and rolled his eyes. "Fine. I won't poke the wolf shifter whose mate is in trouble."

Knox bristled at that and growled a warning, before Bishop sank his fingers into his fur, trying to calm him.

We already knew Audrey was in danger. That was why we were here.

And now I couldn't stop thinking about what would happen if we couldn't convince these men to help. What if this fae sorcerer thought she was too dangerous or couldn't get the evil power out of her? Would he lock her away, or worse, kill her?

They couldn't. I wouldn't let them.

I opened my mouth to tell them that, but Bishop cut me off.

"We've been told you're a fae sorcerer," he said. "Please save our mate. We have money."

He pulled the small purse with the gems out of one of our packs and opened it up so the other men could see.

The guy with horns whistled and the angel cleared his throat.

"They've traveled between realms to save her," Priam said. "They have to be fated mates, Bane."

The fae pinched the bridge of his nose. "And Amiah just got pregnant again."

The angel's face lit up.

"Titus's," the man with horns said.

"Even more amazing," Priam exclaimed. "But we should save—" He paused and glanced at me.

"Audrey," I replied. "Her name is Audrey."

Bishop introduced us, and the fae turned out to be Sebastian Bane and the guy with horns, Hawk.

"Okay," Sebastian said. "I can already tell from here that I can get that shit out of your mate."

"And he has the juice to open a non-fixed gate and send you home," Hawk added, making Sebastian snort even as he started to roll up his sleeves, revealing that his tattoos traveled up to his elbows.

A shadow crossed Bishop's expression, and I almost leaped from the bed and slapped a hand over his mouth. I could see it in his eyes. He was going to tell them the truth.

But then I remembered these beings might be able to

tell if we were lying. We just didn't know anything about them or their abilities.

"The gates to our realm were locked because of a curse. It put the most powerful beings to sleep hundreds of years ago," Bishop confessed. "One of the fae was trapped in our realm and she says she's had time to research the curse and it's safe to reopen the gates. But it might take extra magic to get us there."

"If the gates are locked, how did you get here?" Hawk asked.

"Incomplete mating bond," Bishop replied and Hawk's gaze instantly jumped to me.

Hawk gave a solemn nod. "That's what that is."

Stop talking and fix Audrey, Knox snarled in my head.

"Right." Sebastian strode the three steps to Audrey's bedside and set his hands over her heart, thankfully mindful of where he placed his fingers and palms. Then he closed his eyes and light radiated from his shoulder, turning his white shirt see-through and revealing that his arms and chest were covered in tattoos as well.

A moment later his full-body glow flared blindingly bright, brighter than I'd ever seen Whil's, and my eyes watered because I couldn't look away from Audrey.

Whil had said she wasn't a very powerful sorcerer but I hadn't known until now what that really meant. This man radiated brilliant, blinding power, power that I knew could crush all of us with a single word.

As I watched, the muscles in Sebastian's jaw tightened and Hawk grew tense. Black smoke rose from Audrey, jerking and thrashing against an unseen force, straining to get back inside her.

"Come on, you fucker," Sebastian snarled, and he yanked one of his hands up, drawing out a writhing black core the size of a walnut. "There you are."

With a deep breath, he brought his other hand up and smashed the core between his palms. It exploded into smoke that burst apart and vanished.

"Got it," Sebastian hissed as he sagged forward, clutching the edge of the bed to stay upright.

Hawk stepped close and stared at Audrey's chest, his gaze unfocused. "Looks good."

"It's gone?" Bishop asked and I realized Priam must have used his magic on him while I was distracted since his wounds were healed.

Hawk nodded. "All that's left is a perfect shifter with two and a half mating bonds."

Relief flooded me.

Thank the Sisters. Thank all the sleeping gods. Thank anyone and anything. She was safe.

"Is ah—" Bishop looked at Audrey, his eyes glassy, his relief clear. "Is she still cursed. Her wolf was locked away."

"Cursed?" Hawk frowned.

"There was only the curse woven into the evil power," Sebastian said. "Nothing else."

Which meant my mate had broken her curse when she'd found her wolf while fighting Sterling.

More relief washed through me. I would have loved

her whether she had a wolf form or not, but I knew how much not having one had hurt her... that and her white wolf was stunning. I wanted Audrey to meet her.

And even as I thought that, my body burned. My mate was safe and she needed to wake up. I needed to have her, needed her so damned much I couldn't catch my breath.

"Cyrus?" Bishop asked as I felt my wolf take over.

He needed her too and he'd waited too long. He didn't care that she was unconscious, he had to claim her, now now now.

"Fuck," Hawk hissed. "Priam, call Voth. These two need a room, like ten minutes ago. They shouldn't have to seal their bond in here."

"If they used an incomplete mating bond to get here, it shouldn't be affecting him so soon," Priam said as he took his square device from his pocket while also laying a glowing hand over Audrey's heart and healing her. "But you're the incubus. You'd know best."

I had no idea what an incubus was, but he was right. If I didn't get Audrey some place more comfortable, I was going to claim her on this strange, too-narrow bed and she deserved better than that.

AUDREY

I ached, not a screaming, painful ache, just a steady, persistent throb, and my head felt thick, my thoughts muddled. A heaviness dragged at my limbs, making it impossible to open my eyes, so I just lay there, drifting in a dark limbo, lulled by the nothingness in my head.

Whil had said I was absorbing all of Tzanagoth's power and it was putting me to sleep... but I didn't feel asleep. I felt...

I wasn't sure what I felt. Tired? Worn out?

Empty.

I was empty. The pressure that had filled me, that had grown slowly inside me and I hadn't realized was there, was gone. My stomach felt good, no nausea, and nothing burned which meant Tzanagoth's power was gone.

Bishop, Knox, and Cyrus had done it.

But my wildness was gone as well.

A weight squeezed around my heart. I'd feared

removing the evil power would also remove my newfound wolf and alpha power, and now I was back to being me.

It stung to think that I'd been so close to having everything I'd wanted, to have a wolf and to be a normal shifter. The loss of the hope that somehow I'd be complete hurt and sliced deep into my soul.

Someone moved beside me, and I realized I was lying on something soft just as the sweet scent of fresh-cut grass enveloped me. Straining, I peeled my eyes open and fell straight into the warm brown depths of Bishop's eyes. They were dark, his wolf close to the surface of his consciousness, and the green flecks sparkled like stars, mesmerizing me like they always did.

Love and devotion flooded through our mating bond, filling the void inside me and warming my heart.

God, I loved this man so much. He was amazing and kind and welcomed me from the moment I'd fallen into their lives, a terrified, barely alive mess.

He'd fallen in love with me the way I was, without alpha power or a wolf, or hell, barely any self-confidence, and I knew in the depths of my soul that he would love me no matter what did or didn't change with me.

Woven through Bishop's love was Knox's, a ferocious passion that made my soul sing. We'd had a rocky start — to say the least — but he'd become a fierce protector. His bond was edged with worry and I could sense he wasn't as close as Bishop, probably outside, unable to control his wolf or his claustrophobia.

I sent a wave of love and thanks through our bond and felt his worry burst into relief and joy.

"Thank the Sisters you're awake," Cyrus rumbled, his voice low and broken.

I dragged my gaze away from Bishop's to look at Cyrus. He knelt beside the bed, looking absolutely terrible, his expression haggard and exhausted and edged with a biting desperation. It appeared as though he hadn't slept in days, and the urge to hold him, claim him, protect him from whatever had caused his suffering, washed over me like a tidal wave.

He'd risked everything just to save me — even his pack if we couldn't get back to his realm.

My throat tightened. We'd have saved so much suffering if he'd accepted what I'd known from the time after we'd returned from the death goddess's land. He wouldn't be suffering now, and him putting it off hadn't helped because he'd ended up saying the mating vows at the worst possible moment.

Of course, I wasn't free of blame, either. I could have been courageous and made him talk to me. I hadn't said anything because I was afraid and I hadn't known if me thinking we were mates was all in my head.

That, and if we had bonded, we'd have had no way of getting to my realm to find a fae sorcerer... which I guess they had.

And now here we were, him staring at me like a starving man, completely strung out on what I knew was a burning need to seal the mating bond.

Except if he looked that bad how long had I been asleep? It usually took weeks, sometimes months, before the compulsion to seal the mating bond drove the bonded mates crazy.

Although in my case, my bonds had been anything but usual.

"How long was I...?" I asked, my voice rough as if I hadn't spoken in a long time.

"Only a few hours," Bishop replied, gently brushing a lock of hair away from my face.

But if it had only been a few hours, why did Cyrus look so utterly broken?

"Audrey." Cyrus's voice cracked and his expression grew more strained, the muscles in his jaw flexing as he fought to control himself.

"You and Cyrus need to talk." Bishop pressed a soft kiss to my cheek and inhaled, drawing in my scent then stood. "Knox and I will be outside."

I watched my mate leave, my heart aching for him, needing to be close to him — to all my mates — even though I knew Cyrus and I needed to embrace our fate... which would involve very little talking.

The door closed behind Bishop, leaving me alone with Cyrus, and I turned my attention back to him.

His gaze locked on mine, the weight of his pain and desire radiating from him, and I could practically feel the lust pouring off him as he stared at me with an intensity that made my heart race.

"I'm sorry," he whispered, his voice laced with anguish. "I'm so sorry for everything."

And I knew he meant it. He'd humbled himself before, just after Bishop had been poisoned, and I hadn't been sure I could trust him, but I understood him better now. He needed to be in control and he needed to protect everyone. It was a primal instinct that drove him, made him do and say whatever was necessary to get the job done even if it hurt someone's feelings.

I didn't agree with his tactics, but knowing changed how I saw a lot of our interactions.

I also knew he loved me. He'd been desperate when Tzanagoth's power was flooding into me, and I recognized his fear. It was the same ferocious fear I'd felt when Bishop had been poisoned.

He was stubborn and too self-sacrificing, always putting his pack above himself, but in some ways, we were a lot alike. Both of us were willing to give up everything to save someone we loved, and we both had a strong drive to protect those around us.

Cyrus gently cupped my cheek, his touch warm and tender as he looked deep into my eyes.

"I meant every word of our mating vow, Audrey," he confessed, his voice gruff. "I didn't say it because I was protecting my brothers. I said it because it's true. Bonded or not, I would have gone crazy if I'd lost you. You're my fated mate and I want to be a part of your life."

Warmth spread across my chest and sank low within me. I could feel the truth in his words, the intensity of his love, and his need for me. It was everything I'd felt from Bishop and Knox.

It felt like our fates had finally aligned.

"I was a fool to have ignored my wolf and the truth. You are an amazing, kind, caring woman, and I'd be the most blessed man in all the realms if you'd accept me as your mate."

Joy and heartache swirled into the mix of emotions inside me. Joy because he was finally saying what I had known in my soul was true, and heartache because we'd suffered so much fighting against the undeniable truth. My chest tightened with emotions I couldn't contain, and I blinked back tears as I reached up to touch his face, feeling his rough stubble against my fingertips.

"You're mine," I whispered, my voice barely audible as my throat thickened with emotion.

"I am," he murmured back, his gaze filled with certainty and love.

I leaned toward him and he met me halfway, our lips connecting in a sweet, tender kiss that sank, slow and sultry, into the depths of my soul.

A hard knot in my soul, that I hadn't even realized was there, unraveled, and my wildness, the power I'd thought I'd lost forever unfurled within my chest. The power was warm, comforting, and something settled inside me.

I was complete.

I didn't know how, but I was.

Then Cyrus's sensual kiss grew insistent, his soft

exploration becoming strong and demanding, his grip on his control over the urge from the mating bond slipping. An urgency swelled between us, growing stronger and stronger, and I moaned into his mouth.

"Mate with me," I said against his lips.

"Yes."

AUDREY

With a groan, he crawled onto the bed and pinned me beneath his powerful body. The kiss grew hot and consuming, making me gasp for breath and ache with a soul-deep need for him. Every cell in my body yearned for him to be buried within me and locking our souls together as they were meant to be.

"Cyrus—" I moaned even as I dug my fingers into his hair and drew him closer.

He traced his hands down my neck, leaving a trail of tingling warmth as they skimmed over my bare shoulders, across the front of my dress, and teased my nipples with the barest of touches. My back arched, my body begging for more as pleasure shivered down my spine, pooling like molten lava between my thighs.

His kiss was still strong, edged with desperation, but somehow, he'd held onto enough control to torture me with his touch.

Slowly, so damned slowly, he worked one nipple into an aching, tight bud and then began on the other. My breath turned to ragged gasps, caught between our lips, and I burned for more.

His fingers slid lower, inching down my body with a sensual promise, and I'd never wanted to be naked more in my life. The damned dress was in the way of me savoring the slide of his flesh against mine, and certainly going to get in the way when he finally reached my aching core.

At the thought, slick heat billowed between my thighs. I moaned, rubbing them together, but it only made the ache inside me worse.

If I'd somehow been blind to everything between us and my soul's voice, I would have known in this instant that I needed him. My body burned for him, for his power and control and protection. He was mine and I was never letting him go.

"Please," I moaned against his lips, writhing beneath his touch, trying to get him to move his hand between my thighs. "I need you, Cyrus."

"Patience," he growled, a wave of alpha power swirling around me, urging me to obey even as his body trembled with the effort to hold himself back. "I refuse to take you like an animal, like I did in the shower room."

The reminder of the shower room shuddered through me, hot and sensual, making me gasp. That had been hot, wild, possessive sex, and I ached for that. But I could also tell Cyrus needed to show me how much he cared and he wasn't going to do that with a quick fuck — no matter how good it had felt.

I groaned in frustration and he chuckled.

"Grab the rungs on the headboard and don't let go." More alpha power crashed over me, this one a sharp snap that had me raising my hands before I fully realized what I was doing. "You touch me. I stop."

His hand froze on my thigh, too far away from where I wanted it. Just being told I couldn't, made me want to tangle my fingers in his hair again, slide my palms over his back, and tear at the shirt covering his gorgeous, powerful body.

"Do you understand?" he growled, his eyes so dark I wasn't sure if he was in control of his body or his wolf... except if his wolf was in control, he'd already be buried deep inside me.

"Do you think you can hold out if you stop?" I asked, my voice breathy with need.

He glared at me and I tightened my grip on the headboard. Pushing him was a terrible idea. He needed to be in control and right now he was teetering on the edge of disaster. "I understand."

"Good girl," he said, his words shivering pleasure through me. "I'm so proud you accepted me as your mate."

He sat back on his heels, unclipped the dress's catch at the back of my neck, and peeled down the fabric. I squirmed under his gaze as it slid down to my breasts and the hunger in his eyes grew.

"You're so strong in such a beautiful, kind way." With a groan, he dipped forward and flicked his tongue over one nipple then the other, while he reached beneath me and tore through the tie at my back.

My breath hitched and my body thrummed with need.

Touch me. Please, just touch me.

But instead, he inched my dress over my hips and down my legs before tossing it to the floor. Now he knelt at my feet, his breath ragged, his body tense with the effort to hold himself back.

"Come here," I said.

I started to release one of the rungs to urge him closer but saw something flash in his eyes and tightened my grip instead.

"Good girl. So perfect." His gaze dropped to the crux between my thighs, his moss green eyes dark with passion. "Mine."

He pressed his hands against my knees, urging me to open for him, before sliding his palms up the inside of my thighs and burying his nose in my curls. He drew in a deep breath and hummed his pleasure as I ached to reach down and touch him.

Please.

He raked his tongue through my folds, just a brush that swept up my sensitive flesh and flicked against my clit, the sensation jolting the breath from my body.

Oh, yes.

My head fell back and I moaned, liquid fire roaring through my core.

He licked again and again, with harder, longer strokes, making me gasp and moan. I clung to the headboard, my breath heaving with my building need, determined not to let go.

No way in hell was I going to stop this.

My hips started to buck, my core fluttering with the promise of a breathtaking orgasm.

Cyrus growled against me, the rumble vibrating through my flesh and adding fuel to the fire within me.

Oh, yes. More. I needed more but he was keeping me on the edge, teetering on the precipice, his self control mind blowing.

"Cyrus," I begged.

He pushed two fingers inside me and pumped them in and out and sucked on my clit.

Stars flashed behind my lids and my body jerked as glorious bliss exploded inside me, but even as it started to fade, my desire rose again. I needed to seal our bond. He might have started it and I might not have said the vow, but without a doubt a mating bond had formed between us.

Our gazes met and heat rolled between us. With a snarl, he dove up my body, catching himself before he crushed me, and smashed our lips together.

Any control Cyrus might have had was gone. The kiss was hard, ferocious like our kiss in the shower room. I didn't care that his face was covered in my release or that

I could taste myself on his lips and tongue. All that mattered was being impaled on the hard-as-steel cock pressing against my thigh just shy of my entrance.

"Fuck me." I grabbed his hair and yanked his head back enough that I could look him in the eyes. "Now."

My wildness surged and my alpha power crashed into his in an intense dance of need and longing.

"Mine," he snarled as his canines extended.

"Then claim me, alpha," I barked back.

He thrust into me with a powerful stroke, our pelvises slamming together, his massive cock bottoming out inside me. Then he jerked back and did it again.

He pounded into me, hard and fast and wild, and I had no idea if I was mating with Cyrus or his wolf. But it didn't matter. Cyrus and his wolf were one, two halves of the same soul. All shifters had a primal, ferocious core, and this was Cyrus's true self. I knew he could be soft and tender and in control — he'd already demonstrated that — but I also knew a beast lived deep within him. Just like one lived within me.

I snarled and raked my fingers across his back, drawing blood, and he responded by fucking me harder.

Just like in the shower room he was branding himself on me, body and soul, and I loved it. I met him stroke for stroke, my wildness and power roaring and my desire burning through my veins.

"Fuck, Audrey—"

He raised his head and our eyes met. Love and ferocious devotion shone in those moss green orbs and my wolf howled inside me.

"Blessed be the moon and her children, and blessed be this sacred vow," I moaned. "I answer the call and join my soul with you, my fated mate."

A powerful bell *gonged* inside me, resounding through my soul and flooding me with certainty. I screamed my release, all of my muscles contracting and brilliant light blazing across my vision. Bliss roared through my body, every nerve firing at once, and my wildness, *my wolf*, howled with victory.

With a guttural roar, Cyrus found his own release, his hot seed spilling deep inside me, and he jerked his head to my shoulder, the one without Bishop and Knox's mating marks, and sank his teeth into my flesh.

Another orgasm tore through me as our bond locked into place and I sank into ecstasy.

Cyrus was my fate, just like Bishop and Knox were and my soul was now complete.

AUDREY

After Cyrus and I sealed our bond, the four of us spent a few days at Voth's luxurious hotel in a room on the main floor with a set of sliding doors leading to the outside for Knox.

We rested and made love while waiting to hear Sebastian's decision on whether it was safe to open a proper gate to our realm and return, not wanting to contemplate what would happen if he said it wasn't.

Sebastian returned on the afternoon of the fourth day, said he'd done his research and that it was safe to open a proper gate and not just a rip between our realms.

That said, he suggested, and the guys agreed, to keep the gate controlled on this side so our realm wouldn't be flooded with demons, humans, and other supernatural beings with dubious intent.

We returned home half an hour later to find that Deacon, Nova, and the rest of the Mountain and Sea

Alliance had hunted down and killed the rest of the merchants' grimalkins, but had also agreed to wait ten days before moving on with alliance discussions, hoping we would return.

Our pack had thrown a big party in the center of town — our pack members who hadn't known me and the guys might be stuck in another realm forever thinking the party was because we'd put an end to the grimalkin attacks, something I could fully get behind.

After Cyrus and Bishop concluded the alliance business, they'd turned their attention to Velora who'd been held in a cell in the Residence's basement, no doubt seething with anger and resentment. Knox had voted to kill her, saying she was a serious threat to me, but I begged for forgiveness since with my alpha power I could protect myself.

My forgiveness, however, only went so far, and I said Velora had to be banned from the pack and for everyone in the pack to know that she'd threatened to permanently hurt me so she could have Bishop and be a pack alpha... although I suspected given that we'd had an audience when she'd challenged and threatened me, everyone in the pack already knew.

Now, I stood alone in the Residence's sacred grove, the sun high in the sky, casting dappled light through the ring of trees surrounding me. When I fell into this realm, I'd had nothing — no family, no friends, no safety, and no confidence. I was the girl no one, not even my father wanted, the one Sterling had decided was only good as a human sacrifice so he could gain Tzanagoth's evil power.

But now, I had everything I'd ever wanted. I was safe and loved. I was home.

No one looked down on me and most hadn't cared that I'd had no alpha power and couldn't shift, which still stunned me.

Being around my pack and having them look to me for guidance still made me want to hide — because it was really hard to kick an old habit that had kept me alive most of my life — but I pushed through my discomfort, and most of the pack members were understanding if I was awkward. With that and my mates' love, my confidence grew every day, and I knew someday I'd be able to fully embrace my new life.

A new life that included my wolf.

I was so happy about that. My wolf had finally woken.

Through my own strength of will, and Tzanagoth's power, I'd broken my curse. I was no longer waiting for the right moment and aching because a part of my soul was forever out of reach.

I was complete, just like I was supposed to be.

With a deep breath, I used my newly enhanced senses to take in the smell of the damp earth and the vibrant greenery, the sound of wind rustling through the leaves, and the feeling of sunlight warming my skin. Everything was richer, deeper, brighter, warmer, crisper, perfect.

I slipped out of my dress, leaving it in a heap on the

ground, and, as if I'd been doing it all my life, shifted into my white wolf form.

My first time shifting — when I hadn't been trying to stay alive — had been awkward. I hadn't fully believed I could do it, especially since I still didn't radiate any alpha power until I consciously thought about drawing it out.

But the guys had encouraged me, eager to show me my wolf form, telling me she was beautiful. And she was beautiful. She was easily half the size of the guys' wolves, with delicate paws, ears, and snout, golden eyes, and a stunning, all-white coat.

"Mate," a familiar voice rumbled from behind me as Knox, in his human form, stepped out of the deep shade between the trees.

Mate, I thought back, my gaze meeting his as I marveled over how comfortable he looked in his human form.

When we'd first met, he'd refused to shift into a human. We'd been halfway to the death goddess's temple before I'd even known he and Bishop were identical twins.

And now, he stood with a hint of a grin curling his lips, love radiating through our mating bond, and his hands in his pockets.

With his grin heating, Knox pulled his shirt off over his head and dropped his pants, revealing his stunning, powerful body.

God, I never got tired of looking at him, at all my mates if I was being honest.

He released a slow breath, his grin turning into a smirk, and shifted into his massive black wolf.

My wolf danced from one foot to the other in anticipation, knowing we were going to play from the playfulness radiating through our mating bond, and sure enough, Knot sprang forward and nipped at my haunches.

I hopped out of reach and yipped at him. The game had begun. My wildness rose up, filling me with joyful abandon, and I raced out of the sacred grove with Knox at my heels.

I darted and slipped through the gardens, always avoiding Knox's nips or attempts to pin me. Delight rushed through my veins, feeding off of Knox's happiness, becoming a wonderful, amazing loop of elation.

Knox barked and Bishop in wolf form joined the chase. I raced around the fountain in front of the Residence with the guys hot on my heels. They were bigger than me and could easily beat me in a fight, but I was faster and more nimble.

I careened around the edge of the Residence, barely noticed Cyrus in his wolf form right in front of me, and skidded between his legs before leaping through a narrow slit between a hedgerow.

Well played, Cyrus praised as he leaped over the hedgerow and joined the chase.

I led them on a twisting path through the gardens and around the back of the Residence, evading playful nips and tackles, the joy shifting into something hotter and deeper.

The sensation unfurled through our bonds, heating my soul, and I bounded around the shrubs partially hiding the small patio outside my suite. Between one step and the next, I shifted into my human form and threw open the doors.

Bishop rushed up behind me, also shifting, and scooped me up into his arms, making me laugh with pure joy as the heat within me turned sultry and sank to my core. He bolted through the sitting room into the bedroom and tossed me onto the bed.

With a growl, he dove between my legs, licking and sucking and stealing my laughter, replacing it with pure, burning lust. Knox bounded into the room a second later and captured my lips in a ferocious kiss.

Heat roared in my core, my body instantly aching for my mates as their need flooded me.

"That's it," Cyrus said with a smirk as he sat in a chair near the bed, grabbed his cock, and gave it a slow, hard pump. "I want to hear her scream."

His dark hungry gaze locked on me being ravished by his brothers, and desire shivered from my toes up my body into my scalp.

I moaned as Bishop swiped his tongue over my clit, my pulse pounding, my need screaming for them. I wanted them now, all of them, inside me, filling me, driving me crazy, and making me scream.

Knox tangled his fingers in my hair and raked his

tongue against mine, kissing me as if he couldn't get enough — and from our mating bond I knew he couldn't, just like I couldn't.

One of his hands dropped to my breast, roughly kneading the sensitive flesh and turning my nipple into a taut aching bud while Bishop flicked his tongue over my clit sending bolts of pleasure jerking me closer and closer to the edge until I crashed over, shivering and breathless.

"Oh," I breathed making Bishop grin at me.

"That's what I like to hear," he purred as Knox rolled onto his back and pulled me on top of him. The heat and hardness of his cock pressed against my slit and with one powerful thrust, he plunged inside. A rippling aftershock rolled up my body, and I released a throaty moan.

"Fuck," Knox groaned before he gripped my hips, pulled back, and thrust in again and again.

Need burned through my veins, sweeping me right to edge of another orgasm, but then he stopped, his cock buried inside me.

I moaned in frustration even as my pulse picked up in anticipation. Up to this moment, both Knox and Bishop had played with my puckered entrance, getting me ready for one of them, and I knew the moment was now. I was finally going to have both of them inside me and I couldn't wait.

"Ready, mate?" Knox asked, his voice a low seductive growl as he drew me forward so that I lay against his chest.

"Oh, yes," I groaned, my pulse pounding in my ears, my whole body tingling with aching need.

Bishop swiped his fingers through my wetness and rubbed it against my hole, working in one finger, then two, and turning my desire to molten lava.

I yearned for him, for both of them, for all of them, and I knew I always would. These were my mates. Mine. And I hungered for them.

I trembled against Knox, my body trying to writhe against Knox's firm grip, needing more, needing all of Bishop not just his fingers.

"You're doing so beautifully," Cyrus cooed, pulling my attention to him. "But I still haven't heard you scream."

Need filled his expression and precum glistened at the tip of his cock, making my mouth water for a taste of him.

"You're so fucking sexy, Audrey." Cyrus's eyes darkened, his wolf pushing closer to the surface and his lust roaring through our mating bond. "But Bishop, you're moving too fast. We want our mate to enjoy this."

I groaned and Bishop hummed with pleasure. His fingers slowly pulled out of me and he teased my hole before slowly, achingly slowly, pushed his fingers back in.

My breath stalled, and my desire twisted tighter. I'd almost been on the precipice of another amazing orgasm and my whole body thrummed with the need for a release, but Bishop was an expert at edging me... and apparently Knox too because he was practically vibrating beneath me, his breath short and sharp as he fought to stay still and in control.

The thrumming turned into a burning, a desperate need as Bishop tortured me with slow sensual thrusts.

"Please," I whimpered, desperate for release even though I knew Bishop wouldn't let me come until Cyrus said so.

"Patience, love," Cyrus said, his voice deliciously dark.

I trembled and panted, every touch and sensation amplified as I tried to writhe between my two mates and failed because of Knox's grip on me.

Please. Oh please oh please oh please.

I needed faster, harder, pressure, plunging. I needed it all now now now.

"Patience," Cyrus repeated, his voice a low growl that sent shivers down my spine. I could feel the wolf lurking beneath the surface, ready to take control.

Finally, with my body strung so tight I thought I'd burst, hell, I *needed* to burst, Cyrus gave Bishop the nod.

Thank God.

I felt the hard press of his cock against my hole, adding pressure, until he slipped between the tight ring of muscle and carefully, inch by inch giving me time to adjust, pushed inside me.

Oh.

Oh oh oh.

It was all I could think. There was a bit of a burn, and definitely a stretch, and I was full, so damned, wonderfully full, and the rest was glorious sensation.

A small orgasm rippled through me. I moaned, the sound low and throaty, making all my guys groan, and a shudder of pleasure rolled up my body.

"Sisters, Audrey, you're incredible," Cyrus breathed, sending more desire unfurling inside me.

He rose from the chair, his powerful muscles bunching and flexing with the movement as he strode the few steps to the bed. Bishop pulled out to just the tip and Cyrus brushed his fingers down my spine. It was just a tease of a touch, stealing my breath and making me burn with need.

I shuddered and both Knox and Bishop groaned at the sensation.

"Now open up for me, beautiful," Cyrus commanded.

Without hesitation, I opened my mouth, allowing Cyrus to sink his cock inside, hitting the back of my throat. I moaned around him, and he gripped my hair to keep me steady, then he began slow, languid thrusts into my mouth.

Knox and Bishop joined in, pumping into me, and oh God, it was amazing. Incredible. I never wanted it to stop.

With every thrust, I felt their love and desire pouring through our mating bonds which made my own need spiral higher and higher. I teetered on the edge of release, my body burning, lava flowing through my veins.

I needed— I needed—

The guys plunged into me faster and faster, each thrust growing harder giving me exactly what I craved for.

Then a powerful, screaming orgasm tore through me. I screamed like Cyrus wanted and bliss roared through my veins, sending me spinning into ecstasy.

Bishop slammed home inside me and came, grunting with his release. Knox came a second later with a roar, their cocks throbbing as they pumped me full with their seed. Finally, Cyrus groaned between gritted teeth, and his hot, salty cum flooded my mouth.

I swallowed as best I could, but it was like a faucet had been opened all the way and cum dripped down my chin.

Cyrus's deep earthy scent, along with Bishop's bright fresh-cut grass and Knox's rich wood smoke enveloped me. Pride and love flooded my mating bonds, sending another mini orgasm rushing through me, leaving me breathless and floating in a sea of euphoria.

In this moment, I knew I was truly loved and cherished by my mates, and I couldn't imagine a more beautiful feeling.

I WOKE THE NEXT DAY, MY BODY ACHING IN ALL THE RIGHT ways, and peace radiating around my heart. My back was to Cyrus's chest, his arm wrapped protectively around me, and I stared at Bishop's beautiful face, his expression relaxed with sleep.

My lips curled in a smile as I remembered how

amazing yesterday afternoon and last night had been. After having all my guys at once, we'd dozed before waking and making love again... before dozing and waking again.

It was no wonder the sunlight streaming through the windows was mid-morning bright.

I stretched, savoring the ache between my legs and connected with Knox's mating bond to see where he was. He'd left just as the sun was rising after being able to control his claustrophobia for longer than he ever had before. But instead of feeling any regret for leaving, all I felt from him was contentment.

That made my smile deepen, and I carefully eased from Cyrus's embrace and wiggled out from the blankets then down to the end of the bed to avoid waking my mates. Cyrus huffed in his sleep and Bishop frowned as if they could tell, even while unconscious, that I was moving away from them.

But I wasn't going far. I could sense Knox just outside my suite and I wanted some cuddles from my gruff mate before everyone else was around.

Free from the bed, I tiptoed to my wardrobe, picked a simple dress, and secured it behind my neck and around my back, not caring that it showed off almost all of my scars.

As much as I hated that I was covered in those perma-nent marks, something no other shifter had, I also now recognized them for what they were: proof that I was a survivor, that I was strong enough to get through anything, even being sacrificed to a man-eating monster-god.

I hurried out of the bedroom to the French doors in the sitting room, and stepped onto the patio. Knox, in his human form, stood on the edge, his eyes closed, his face tipped up to the sun, basking in it. He wore one of the kilt-like wraps that were popular in Stonehaven and nothing else, and I couldn't help but appreciate his powerful, sculpted back and arms.

A soft sigh escaped me — God my mates were stunning — and he turned to face me, a rare smile tugging at his lips, softening his expression.

"Mate," he growled, and he pulled me into his strong arms and pressed his nose against the top of my head, breathing in my scent.

Rich wood smoke enveloped me and I sank into his embrace. I'd loved his scent from the moment I'd smelled it, even before I'd known it was from the man I'd accidentally mate bonded with.

With one more deep breath, Knox drew away, leaving me aching for his warmth.

"Come," he said. "I have a surprise."

"Really?" I asked.

Knox wasn't a surprise kind of guy. Bishop was. But that only made me more curious.

He nodded and took my hand, leading me away from the front of the Residence and around a corner to a narrow side door.

"Close your eyes," he instructed.

"Close—?"

"Bishop said you had to close your eyes," he huffed, making me giggle and proving that Bishop had a hand in whatever was going on.

I closed my eyes, and with my hand in his, Knox opened the door, guided me inside, and up what felt like an endless flight of stairs that kept going around and around.

When we stopped, another door's hinges squeaked, and we stepped outside. Warm sun heated my face and bare shoulders and a gentle breeze caressed my skin. The scent of the Residence's gardens mingled with something that smelled amazing and familiar but I couldn't quite place, and I could hear voices somewhere, but not tell what they were saying.

"Open your eyes," Knox said, and I obeyed, my breath catching in my throat.

We stood on the Residence's roof, the flat area before me stretching between one of the turrets and a sloped section of the roof.

I turned around, soaking in the breathtaking view of the Residence's grounds and the town beyond the Residence's walls.

Holy smokes, the view was amazing.

Then it hit me. This was a flat area on the roof, more than big enough for a bedroom. Were the guys going to make my dream of a greenhouse bedroom reality?

"Is this...?" I asked.

"It is." Knox grinned back at me. "Your greenhouse bedroom."

"It's going to be amazing," I said, throwing myself at Knox.

He caught me and hoisted me up so I could wrap my legs around his waist. Our lips crashed together and I released all my love and joy into our kiss.

I knew the guys loved me, but that didn't mean my greenhouse bedroom would be a reality. Engineers had to be consulted, weather patterns, and a whole bunch of other things, not to mention taking money from the pack to add a room to the Residence just for me.

"So," Bishop said, startling me and breaking my kiss with Knox. "What do you think?"

He and Cyrus stood in the doorway and I grinned at them.

"I think it'll be amazing." Images of what it could be flitted through my mind. I could already see it, reading nooks hidden by greenery, part of the roof not enclosed for a balcony, and a bed in the center, big enough for the four of us.

"Why don't we get brunch and talk about what needs to be done," Cyrus suggested, his words calm despite the hum of anticipation thrumming through our bond.

I raised my eyebrow at him in question and he raised his eyebrow back at me, refusing to answer.

Something was up, but none of Cyrus's feelings were bad so I was happy to wait... at least until my curiosity got the better of me.

Together, we descended the stairs and stepped outside the Residence, ensuring Knox could stay with us for as long as possible. Bishop laced his fingers with mine, giving me his most brilliant, heart stopping smile and I grinned back at him.

We strolled around the back, toward the herb garden and the kitchen's back door, but I stopped at the sight of a large table. It sat in the only open area in the herb garden and was surrounded by chairs and people. Platters piled high with pastries, fruit, eggs, bacon, and sausages awaited us, and I realized it was the amazing smell I'd detected earlier while standing on the roof.

But what really made me pause were the people. Everyone I cared for was there, Eloise and Kira putting the finishing touches on the table, Quinn and Zavier helping them, while Nova, Deacon, and Lucius chatted.

Quinn noticed us first and rushed toward me.

"Happy birthday!" she said before wrapping me in a tight hug.

I hugged her back, stunned. A while back, I'd mentioned I had a birthday coming up. I didn't remember how it had come up in conversation, but I never expected her to remember or make a fuss, especially with everything that had happened.

"I'm not sure if today is the actual day, but from what you said, I figured today was close enough." She stood back, her expression bright.

"This is amazing," I replied. "Thank you."

Tears welled in my eyes as warmth spread through

me. No one had ever celebrated my birthday before —
not even my father. Yet here were my new friends, my
family, making it seem like the most natural thing in the
world even though they'd only known me for a few
months.

Bishop spun me around and pressed a deep, sensual
kiss on my lips, leaving me heated and breathless.

"We've got an amazing day planned for the four of
us," he told me. "Starting with one of Eloise's incredible
brunches."

He spun me around, right into Knox's arms who
captured my mouth with his usual ferocious passion,
adding to the heat building inside me.

If the guys kept this up, I was going to need to skip
breakfast.

When I was nearly gasping for air, and melting in
Knox's arms, Cyrus pulled me into his embrace, but
instead of kissing me, he brushed his lips against my
cheek, sending a shiver of anticipation rushing
through me.

"And I've got something special saved for you at the
end of the night."

Oh, boy. Could we just skip to dessert?

Cyrus's gaze heated and everyone else laughed,
making my cheeks flush with embarrassment.

Guess they heard that.

It's okay, beautiful, Bishop said in my mind. *We all
know you're still figuring out your telepathy.*

And they did. Everyone had been so kind and understanding as I figured out my new abilities.

I'd never felt so loved before, and while it helped that I could feel my mates' love and devotion through our mating bonds, it was more than that. It was how they treated me with kindness and generosity, and how my new friends did the same.

This was where I belonged.

I'd finally found my place, my pack, my mates, and the people who loved and accepted me for who I was.

I'd finally found home.

OTHER BOOKS BY TESSA COLE

THE NEPHILIM'S DESTINY SERIES

Destined Shadows, prequel story

Destined Darkness, book 1

Destined Blood, book 2

Destined Fire, book 3

Destined Storm, book 4

Destined Radiance, book 5

THE ANGEL'S FATE SERIES

Fated Bonds, book 1

Fated Winter, book 2

Fated Fear, book 3

Fated Despair, book 4

Fated Resolve, book 5

Fated Heart, book 6

THE GRECIAN GODDESS TRILOGY

Written with Clara Wils

Kiss of the Goddess, book 1

Power of the Goddess, book 2

Bonds of the Goddess, book 3

ENSNARED BY THE PACK

Wolf Deceived, book 1

Wolf Denied, book 2

Wolf Desired, book 3

Wolf Distressed, book 4

Wolf Decided, book 5

Wolf Devoted, book 5

SECRETS GODS KEEP

Written with Clara Wils

Craving Demons, book 1

Chaos Demons, book 2

Claiming Demons, book 3